This is a work of fiction. All of the characters, organizations, and events portrayed in this novel are either products of the author's imagination or are used fictitiously.

Wifey 4 Life. Copyright © 2010, 2012 by Kiki Swinson. All rights reserved. Printed in the United States of America. No part of this book may be used or reproduced in any manner whatsoever without written permission except in the case of brief quotations embodied in critical articles or reviews. For information, address Melodrama Publishing, P.O. Box 522, Bellport, NY 11713.

www.melodramapublishing.com

Library of Congress Control Number: 2009938152

ISBN-13: 978-1934157435

ISBN-10: 1934157430

Mass Market Edition: February 2012

10 9 8 7 6 5 4 3 2 1

Interior Design and Layout by candacecottrell.com

Cover Design by Marion Designs

Cover Model: Gabriella

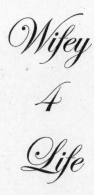

Wifey 4 Life

KIKI SWINSON

Buy

for Melodrama

LIVING AT PEACE

The sound of my BlackBerry ringing woke me out of a dead sleep. I started to get up to see who it was, but my mind wouldn't allow my body to move, so I lay there, hoping it would stop ringing on its own. A couple of seconds later I felt Donovan rub me on my back while I had my face buried underneath my pillow.

"Want me to answer this?"

Before I answered, the phone stopped ringing.

"It was your realtor, Kendra," he told me after looking at the caller ID.

"I'll call her back later," I said, my response barely audible.

"What did you say?"

I sighed and lifted my head from underneath the pillow. The sunlight beaming through the window treatments nearly blinded me, so I squinted and repeated what I'd said. Then I put my head back under the pillow.

"Sweetheart, this is her second time calling. You may want to call her back now."

I thought about what he said for a moment. "Give me ten more minutes and then I'll get up and call her back."

He patted me once again on my back. "OK, I'm giving you ten minutes to get up, because she could be calling you about the inspection."

I started to make a rebuttal to his comment, but I decided against it, because I was too tired to speak, and I didn't have a bit of strength to lift my head again. I just lay there and pretended I hadn't heard him, even though I knew he meant well.

It was funny how Donovan and I were just opposites, yet we meshed like two peas in a pod. Donovan Tate, a native of Anguilla, was more handsome than anyone I'd ever been intimate with. What attracted me to him was his big, brown eyes and perfect white teeth.

The day we met on the beach not too far from my house, he'd approached me and introduced himself while I lounged in my chair reading a book by one of my favorite authors. He walked barefoot in the sand with a cute little poodle in tow. When I looked at him from head to toe, he didn't strike me as the type of man who'd own a poodle. So when he told me the dog belonged to his parents, who lived a few houses up the beach from my place, it made perfect sense.

I honestly couldn't believe him when he told me he was in his late twenties. I swear I would've bet every dime I had that he was my age or a couple of years older. His height and his build tipped him over the thirty-something scale. He wasn't as tall as Shaquille O'Neal, but he was damn near close. And although I never asked him how much he weighed, I was sure he was every bit of 280 pounds. The good thing about it was that he carried his weight well, and without a stitch of flab on his entire body, he was solid as a rock.

Lucky for him, the king-sized bed I had in my bedroom was big enough to hold him, because if I had anything smaller, he'd be sleeping on the floor.

We'd been dating for a month, and so far it'd been one incredible journey.

I had my doubts in the beginning when he first pursued me, but after I met his parents, I knew then that God had His hands in this one. They were poised, successful, and they embraced me wholeheartedly. All the other men I'd chosen in the past—every single one of them—came with all sorts of drama. That was why I'd given up the hope that I'd ever find true love.

But Donovan was different. He did everything in his power to make me happy. Plus, he was an excellent cook.

Two weeks ago the sink in my kitchen got clogged up, and before I could lift a finger to call a plumber, he got underneath that sink, disconnected the pipes, removed the debris, and screwed the pipes back together. He handled his business like a professional. Which saved me a few coins. I knew he was heaven-sent.

I lay in bed past the time I had promised to Donovan, so he sat back on the bed and massaged me on my back. I knew he was about to remind me about my commitment to call Kendra back. He was a stickler when it came to taking care of important business, unlike me. I was a procrastinator, so we bumped heads when it came to that. I lay there very still and hoped that he'd leave me alone. I knew it would be a long shot, but I tried my hand anyway.

"Baby, it's time to get up," he said. "Remember, you got to call Kendra back."

Dreading to move even one inch, I stretched out my hands from under the covers and let out a long yawn. I was exhausted, and I made sure he knew it. "Baby, can you give me at least ten more minutes?" I whined, my head still buried beneath the pillow.

"No, it's time to get up!" He reached his hand under the blanket and eased it up the back of my legs until he located my ass.

I knew what he was about to do. He loved to fondle me when I gave him a hard time about getting out of bed. He definitely knew how to get my attention.

I waited for the inevitable, and then it happened—the gentle touch of Donovan's hands massaging my butt and my inner thighs. I spread my legs apart slowly and started getting moist instantly.

When he felt the wetness through my panties, he started playing with my kitty cat. I swear, my insides wanted to burst. And since I couldn't resist him any longer, I slowly turned over on my back and spread my legs even farther apart.

At that very moment he yanked my panties so hard, he ripped them completely off me, leaving my bare coochie showing, and went in for the kill.

I moaned and groaned with every lick he laid upon me, arching my back and purring like a fucking cat. "Yeah, baby, lick right there," I said. Believe me, the shit felt good as hell. I belted out a couple of screams of ecstasy.

Donovan concentrated on that exact spot of my clit and went crazy.

"Ahhhhh, baby, yeah. Yeah, please don't stop." I moaned and gripped the sides of his ears. I wasn't gonna let them go for nothing in the world.

I was almost at my peak when my BlackBerry started ringing again. I tried not to listen to it because I knew it would distract me from getting an orgasm. But it kept ringing and ringing. I felt Donovan's tongue stop moving.

"What are you doing? You can't stop now."

"The call is probably important."

"I don't give a damn about that phone right now. I need you to make me cum."

Donovan wasn't trying to hear it. He stood and grabbed my phone from the dresser. "Here, take care of your business first. I can make you cum anytime."

I was pissed with that motherfucker for starting some shit with me that he wouldn't finish. My pussy was so wet, you could soak up my juices with a mop and use it to clean the entire kitchen floor. And to think it was all done for nothing. Boy, what a fucking waste.

I finally answered the phone, but I wasn't a happy camper at all. "How can I help you?"

"Hi, Kira. This is Kendra. I was calling you to let you know that the inspection on the house went very well, and now all we have to do is get through escrow and then we can go to closing."

"Sounds good," I said nonchalantly. At this point, I really couldn't care less about the fucking inspection. I knew my house was going to pass, because it was practically brand-new. All she needed to do was call me when those people were ready to go to closing.

"Do you think you'll be available to come back here in the next couple of days?" she asked.

"Yeah, I can do that."

"OK, well, book a flight and have yourself here by Tuesday. Today is Saturday, so that gives you three days."

"All right. I'm on it," I assured her, and then we hung up.

After I got off the phone with Kendra, I was no longer in the mood to have Donovan get back on his knees, so I got out of bed and headed to the shower. I figured what I really needed was some hot water beating down my back, and that was what I got.

When I got out of the shower, I went back into my bedroom and slipped on one of Donovan's white tank tops and a pair of my own jean shorts. Down here in Anguilla, they called these shorts "coochie-cutters." I loved the way I looked in them. And Donovan loved the way I looked in them even more.

After I slipped on a pair of my Gucci flip-flops, I took my ass downstairs to see where Donovan was. He wasn't in the kitchen like I expected him to be, but I did find him relaxing on his favorite chair in the family room of my home. He had the remote control in his hand, surfing the channels to see what was on.

I gave him a half-smile, because, for one, I was still kind of ticked off that he left me hanging in the bedroom. And, two, I knew that when I walked in here and he smiled at me, I wouldn't be mad at him much longer. He always knew how to make me get over any mishaps he and I had, which was what drew me to him in the first place. No matter how much he and I argued or fussed, he would never allow us to go to bed angry. That was why I knew he was my soul mate.

"You hungry?"

I tried to play hard, but it didn't work. "No, I'm fine." I flopped down on the sofa across from him.

He got up from his chair and took a seat beside me. "You know I don't like it when you aren't happy."

"I'm happy."

"Stop lying to me. You know I know when you're not telling me the truth," he said, and then he started tickling me.

I burst into laughter. "Stop playing, Donovan. You know I hate when you be tickling me." I screamed and chuckled at the same time.

"I'm not gonna stop until you tell me the truth." He continued tickling me.

The shit was unbearable. I couldn't contain myself for all the money in the world. I was getting weaker by the second, and I couldn't do a thing about it. "OK. OK. I'ma stop lying and tell you the truth."

When he heard my surrender, he immediately stopped. "You promise?"

I smiled. "Yes, I promise."

He released his hands from my side, and I exhaled. He kissed me on my forehead and asked me what I wanted for breakfast.

"I'm not really hungry, baby, but you can fix me a cup of hot tea."

"All right. I gotcha covered."

I watched him as he exited the room. I sat back and thought to myself how lucky I was to have that man in my life. He was such a sweetheart, and the fact that he showed me how much he loved me in such a short time, especially with all my emotional baggage, made me value him even more. I swear, I wouldn't trade him in for nothing else in this entire world. I just wished that he'd come into my life a couple of years earlier. Then I wouldn't be such an emotional wreck. But I knew I'd be all right. God promised me that He'd look after me, so I knew that was exactly what He was going to do.

THE PERFECT MAN

An hour or so after I drank my cup of tea, Donovan decided he wanted to hop on his family's boat and take me to Saint Martin to do some shopping, since I was going back to the States to handle some business. Now when he mentioned Saint Martin, I knew we would be stopping at the Versace and Gucci boutiques, two of my favorite designers, and I made sure he knew that on our first date.

Before we left my house, he encouraged me to change into something more appropriate since he planned to stop by his parents' house on the way back. He told me his mother wanted us over for lunch, which I told him was fine, even though I knew this lunch date with her would turn into a Q and A session. Every time I was in her company, she wanted to know a little bit more about me.

Everything I told her about me was a lie, of course, especially the part about my ex-husband dying in a car accident, and that I'd inherited his insurance policy valued at two million. I also told her that I owned an exclusive hair, nail, and body spa geared toward the elite back in America, and netted a profit of three hundred thousand yearly. The only real thing I told her was my name. I tried not to get so caught up in my lies that I didn't remember them later, so I always tried to keep everything at a minimum.

Other than his mom's nosiness, both of Donovan's parents were very sweet people. They loved me from the first day they met me. Well, maybe his father loved me more. I found him staring at me on several occasions. He'd even made a comment about how lucky his son was, and that if he was younger, he would've liked to have had me too.

I laughed it off. Little did he know, if I wasn't involved with his son, and he wasn't married, I would've gotten with him, especially since he was handsome and established.

Donovan had told me how long his father's money was. He said that his dad used to be an investment banker, that he and Donovan's mother owned a lot of land and real estate in Anguilla. I was really impressed.

His mother was a retired schoolteacher, so she lived day to day doing absolutely nothing. I envied her just a tad bit, because she seemed like she was the happiest woman alive. No drama at all. And she appeared not to have any hang-ups, which I liked the most about her.

Donovan's mom and dad were both of light brown complexion, and very tall. He had to be at least six feet and some change. He and Donovan were almost the same height. And his mother came in only a couple of inches shorter. I looked like a midget compared to them. But it was cool, because they were very nice people and they understood what loyalty meant. So my guess was, I was gonna be around for the long haul. Well, at least until I saw differently.

The boat ride to Saint Martin was beautiful and serene. I couldn't have asked for a better life. Not only did I have plenty of money to live on, but Donovan and his family had plenty of dough too. That meant I didn't have to spend mine. And I loved every bit of that picture, especially if he and I decided to get married. I would be set for life. And the best part about all that was, it was all legit. No hustling. No FBI. No narcotics detectives investigating him. And I didn't have to worry about niggas hiding out and plotting to kidnap me for ransom. Now how much better could it get?

The moment we docked in Saint Martin at least five little boys rushed toward the boat to help Donovan tie the rope to the metal hook, to make a few coins to take back home to their parents. These little hustlers-in-the-making knew how to get it from the rough, and I respected them for it.

Donovan gave all of them a few bucks, and they scattered like roaches. "What store you want to go in first?" he asked me.

"Why? Is there a particular store you want to go in first?"

"No, baby. But I would like to stop off at the Cigar Emporium and pick up a box of Cuban cigars for my father before we leave."

I grabbed his hand. "Well, let's go take care of that now."

He smiled at me. "You are so sweet!"

I smiled back and winked at him. After we picked up a box of his father's favorite cigars, we raided the Gucci store first, and then the Versace. The saleswoman in the Gucci store was very nice to us. But when we stepped foot inside the Versace store, I felt a thick cloud of hate hovering over my head. Every salesperson in there was gritting on me like they hated my fucking guts. Shit, I didn't know them, and they didn't know me. So I wondered why they were throwing shade at me.

While Donovan and I looked at their shoe selection, I heard whispering not too far from where we were standing. I turned around to see who was doing the whispering and noticed two dark-skinned chicks in a huddle, staring at me. I couldn't understand what they were saying because their words were barely audible, but from their facial expressions, I was certain they were talking shit about me.

Now I wanted to confront them but decided against it. I didn't want Donovan to see the ghetto side of me. And, besides, if I acted out like a complete idiot, then they would have won the battle.

I decided to pull Donovan's coat about what they were doing. He looked back at them and smiled. I thought he was going to say something to them about it, but the next thing I know, he was summoning them like they were servants.

"Oh, ladies, can you come here, please? We need you both to help us with these shoes over here," he told them.

Both of those tired-looking witches scrambled over to us. "How can we help you?" one of them asked.

Donovan turned toward the shoes and pointed to at least ten different pairs. "She needs to see all of these in a size eight and a half."

Both women looked at him, and then they looked at each other. "You want to see all of those?" the same woman asked.

"Yes. She wants to see all of those shoes in a size eight and a half."

"OK, we will be right back," the woman replied, and then they both hurried away.

I looked at Donovan. "Why did you tell them to get me all ten of those shoes? I only liked four of them."

He pulled me into his arms and held me tightly. "I only did it to see the expression on their faces. And it was priceless." He smiled and kissed me on the forehead. "The reason why they were staring at you and making those ugly facial gestures is because they're jealous of you."

"You think so?"

"Kira, look at you. You are beautiful. Any woman in their right mind wouldn't dare compete against you."

I smiled bashfully. "Oh, stop it, Donovan."

"But it's the truth, baby. And, besides that, most Caribbean women are jealous of American women, especially a woman of your complexion, because you stick out even more. And to see you with a Caribbean man who is well-off makes them even more jealous."

"Well, I hope I never run into one of those crazy

chicks who wants to throw acid in my face because she's in love with you."

"You wouldn't ever have to worry about anything like that. I'm gonna always be by your side to protect you."

I looked up at him with an expression of uncertainty. After a few seconds I smiled and said, "I'm gonna hold you to that."

ATTENDING THE LUNCHEON

Our shopping excursion lasted another hour and then we got back on the boat and traveled the twenty minutes back to Anguilla. We dropped off our bags at my house, and then we hurried over to his parents' house. Their home was beautiful. Like mine, it was a two-story home with huge louver windows. Mrs. Tate didn't have window treatments, so you could see inside. I thought it was very tasteful, but the way my life had always been, to allow people to look into my house at their leisure would've given me a creepy feeling. I needed my privacy.

When we entered his parents' home, his mother was placing food on the dining room table, while his father sat at the table and watched. I greeted them both and took a seat at the table. Donovan asked his mother if she needed any help, but when she told him no and to take a seat at the table, he did just that. He and his father made small talk, while his mother made preparations for us to eat.

I commented on how good the food smelled, which put a smile on her face.

"Thank you, darling," she replied. And then she asked

me if I ever had steamed red snapper with callaloo and sweet potatoes. I told her I did, but I refused to tell her that I was introduced to that dish by my late husband. I'd always tried not to tell them anything about my past, since Ricky was a huge part of it. I did tell her that my favorite Caribbean dish was ackee and saltfish, which she promised to cook for me the following morning.

Lunch was very good. That woman could cook her butt off. I asked her to teach me how to cook like that, and she assured me she would.

After lunch Donovan and his father went outside to talk, which left me in the house, and his mother could have her way with me. Sometimes I felt uncomfortable when she would put me on the hot seat. I hated her Q and A sessions, which seemed to last forever and a day.

Donovan had to save me a couple of times, but I really didn't see that happening this time. I knew she only questioned me to see what my motives were and to see if I was fit to be with her son, which was only natural. If I were in her shoes, I would do the same thing.

"You know Donovan wants to have children, right?"

"Yes, I know. Remember you and I talked about this before?"

"Has he told you how many he wanted?"

"Yes, ma'am."

"Are you willing to have that many?"

I smiled, thinking back to the day Donovan told me he wanted to have at least five kids, since he was an only child and often felt lonely growing up.

"I told him I wasn't comfortable having that many kids, but I could probably meet him in the middle."

"That's a nice way to come to a happy medium," she commented. "Well, this is supposed to be a surprise, but I must let you know that he plans to propose to you as soon as you come back from the States."

Totally caught off guard, I sat there motionless.

"Are you all right?" she asked me.

Trying to absorb what she had just told me, I said, "Yes, I'm fine. I'm just trying to take in everything you just told me."

She didn't hesitate to ask, "What are your thoughts?"

Honestly, I was having mixed feelings, but I wouldn't tell her that. I didn't want her to know about all the drama I'd experienced in my last marriage that caused me withdraw from the subject of weddings. I did, however, love her son, but at this particular moment I didn't feel like I was ready to be engaged to him. I wanted to take my time with our relationship, not wanting to rush into anything like I did with Ricky and what I was about to do with Fatu'.

So I sat there in my chair, looked into Mrs. Tate's eyes, and lied. "I would love to marry your son, but I'm still mourning the loss of my late husband."

"Well, that's understandable. In situations like that, sometimes it takes some people longer to get over a loved one, but in this case, all Donovan wants to do is get engaged. So would you accept his proposal?"

"Ummmm . . . yes, I would."

"I sensed a little hesitation in your answer. Are you sure? Because I would hate to see my son get let down."

"I wouldn't let down your son, Mrs. Tate. I love him too much to do that to him."

"Well then, it's settled. You and he will get engaged when you return from the States, and we're gonna have a big celebration." She stood and clapped her hands together. "Now all I have to do is call all the relatives." She walked over to the kitchen drawer to pull out her address book.

I sat there and watched the excitement on her face. I could see it now. She was gonna try to plan our fucking wedding.

WAITING ON THE PHONE CALL

Kendra called me back to follow up with me on the progression of the sale of my house. For some reason, though, this call seemed odd. She wasn't being her normal self, so I asked her what was wrong. She gave me a spiel about a deal that fell through. Hoping to raise her spirits, I reminded her that after the paperwork for my house was signed, she would make a large commission, but she brushed off my comment with a fake-ass laugh. Then she quickly asked me what time I would be arriving at the airport. Her behavior seemed odd to me, but I let it go.

"My plane will arrive in Houston at ten thirty-five in the morning. So I'll see you in the a.m."

"Sounds good," she said.

After I ended the call, I headed onto the balcony of my bedroom to find Donovan. He had been out there for at least thirty minutes and looked like he was deep in thought.

"What's on your mind?" I asked him as I took a seat on his lap.

He was sitting on one of my wooden lounge chairs. It sat low to the ground, so it felt like we were sitting on the bare floor. It was sort of uncomfortable for me, so after a few minutes, I sat in the lounge chair beside him.

"I'm just thinking about how lucky I am to have you."

I smiled. "Oh, baby, that is so sweet!" I placed my hand on his knee.

"No, I'm serious, Kira. I've been looking for a woman like you all my life, and now that I finally got you, I feel like my life is complete."

Hearing Donovan pour out his heart to me made me reflect back on the marriage proposal his mother told me he had planned for when I came back from the States. We'd only been together for a little over a month, so for him to think about marrying me was somewhat of a pretty big apple to chew on. He was in his late twenties, financially well situated, and didn't have any children lingering around, so he was a damn good catch.

But in the back of my mind I kept wondering if one of his skeletons would rear its ugly head, and whether, when it did, it would be so bad that I wouldn't be able to handle it. I was tired of running into good prospects, and then after some time passed, the real man came out. I couldn't afford to get hurt again. The next time I'd probably have a fucking nervous breakdown.

While I thought about the what-ifs, Donovan was still pouring out his love for me. He even got down on his knees, which shocked the hell out of me.

Next he went into the left pocket of his shorts and pulled out a black box. I wanted to faint, but I knew I couldn't. My heart did flip a couple of times, and the palms of my hands became sweaty.

I waited patiently for him to pop the question, but since it seemed like everything was going in slow motion, I opened my mouth to say something. But he placed his finger against my lips to prevent me from saying anything. Then he pulled his finger back from my lips and opened the black box. Inside was a beautiful princess cut diamond set in white gold. The diamond almost blinded me.

"I know you and I haven't known each other very long," he began, "but when you're in love like I am in love with you, there's no way I could've put a time limit on when to ask you to marry me. So, will you marry me? And before you answer my question, just take into consideration that I know you're probably still mourning your late husband, so we don't have to get married right away. But please don't count me out, because I promise I will never hurt you, and if we ever have any problems, I promise we will work through them. I would do any and everything to keep us together, because I want to grow old with you."

"I want to grow old with you too," I said, not realizing I had opened my mouth. My heart had overpowered my mind.

"Well, will you marry me then?"

I hesitated for a second, thinking about how long my engagement had lasted with Fatu'. But then I thought about the fact that Donovan had assured me that we didn't have to get married right away, so I smiled at him and said, "Yes, I will marry you."

Donovan's eyes became glassy as he fumbled with the black box. He was having minor problems trying to take the ring out of the box. I sat there patiently and waited for him to get control of the situation. When he finally got it out and slid it on my finger, I looked at it about four or five times at different angles, and then I said, "This is so beautiful. Thank you, baby!"

He leaned over to kiss me. "You're welcome, sweetheart! Now let's go tell my parents the good news."

I stood. "Let me freshen up in the bathroom, and I'll meet you downstairs."

"All right. But don't take too long." He kissed me on the lips right before he walked off.

I watched him as he left my presence. As soon as he left, I rushed into the bathroom and took a seat on the chair in front of my vanity. I know I looked down at the ring another fifty times. It was indeed beautiful, but I could tell that it wasn't as expensive as the rock Fatu' had given me when he'd asked me to marry him. Thank God, we never made it to the altar, because after all the shit I found out about him, I would've probably been the one to kill him, and not his cousin Bintu'.

Now I had to admit, this ring was quite nicer than the diamond Ricky had given me, so I was satisfied. Hopefully if we tied the knot, Donovan would get me an upgrade in a few years. I had to make sure I got with him on that outing so I could help pick it out. I couldn't see it any other way, since I had no choice this time around.

HARSH REALITIES

I should've listened to my first intuition when my realtor back in Houston called me and told me everything was a go. But, no, stupid me went against my better judgment and hopped on the next flight to Texas. What in the world was I thinking? I didn't need the money the so-called couple had offered. I guess I just wanted to move on with my life. Well, thanks to my realtor, that didn't happen. I traveled with my Louis Vuitton carry-on bag so I wouldn't have to make a stop at baggage claim. I planned to fly into Houston, sign whatever paperwork I needed to sign, collect my funds from my realtor, and head back to Anguilla the very next morning. But Houston's homicide detectives had a different plan for my ass.

As soon as I walked off the plane, two white men approached me with their badges in hand and advised me to follow them to the airport's security office. Fear consumed me, and now my mind confirmed what my gut had told me a couple days ago. I knew my bitch realtor had set me up, since she was the only one who knew I was coming to Houston, but there was nothing I could do about it now.

I followed these white men like I was asked, and from there we headed down to their headquarters. They took me to a small room with a metal table and three chairs. There was one of those two-way mirrors on the wall like you saw on those police detective television shows, but that shit didn't faze me one bit. I knew how the game was played. It wasn't like I hadn't been in this type of predicament before. Shit, I'd been in interrogation rooms with some of the best investigators the feds had to offer, so I was thinking, *These little puppies better come correct with whatever they got, or don't come at all.*

It didn't surprise me that those bastards left me in that room for over two fucking hours. I was beyond furious when they marched their asses into the room to start their little interrogation. And even though they hadn't divulged one word about why they were detaining me, I knew it was about my cousin Nikki.

Both detectives took a seat. The fat one was the first one to speak. "Would you like something to drink?" he asked.

I sucked my teeth and gave him the most disgusted expression I could muster. "Do I look like I need something to drink?"

"Ms. Walters, there is no need for the sarcasm. All we're trying to do is make you as comfortable as possible," the fat man replied.

"You can't make me comfortable by sitting in this little-ass room. Let me the hell out of here, and then I'll start to feel comfortable," I roared.

"Ms. Walters, we will let you go as soon as you answer a few questions," the other detective said.

I sighed heavily. "Am I under arrest?"

"No, ma'am, you're not," the same detective said.

"So, why did you bring me all the way down here? Don't you think I've got better shit to do than to be locked up in some cold-ass room?"

The fat detective said, "I'm sure you do, Ms. Walters, but we are investigating your cousin's murder, and—"

"My cousin's murder? What are you talking about?" I asked, trying to act as shocked and distraught as I could. I knew I had to put on my acting hat, because these motherfuckers were looking at my body language and my facial expressions really hard, so they were ready for me to slip up. I wasn't going to let that happen. I had too much riding on my freedom. I wasn't going to let these bastards lock up my ass for being an accessory to her murder. Not only that, if they had the slightest inclination that I knew the motherfuckers who actually killed her, they would use it against me and try to get me to rat them out. Now how the hell would that look? I would be right back in fucking court testifying against another set of foreigners. And those African cats seemed like they were a little crazier than Papi and his boys. So I might not have the luxury of getting away this time.

And what made the shit even worse was that I wouldn't be able to get back into the Witness Protection Program. When I'd elected to leave that nest the last time, I'd forfeited my chances of ever hiding under its umbrella again. So if these assholes thought I was gonna start singing like a bird for the second time around, they had another think coming. I was going to play the I-don't-know-shit card and see how far that took me.

"Your cousin Nikki was murdered," the fat detective replied.

Thinking about the pain Nikki suffered before she was murdered by Bintu' wasn't enough to bring me to tears. With all the unnecessary drama I went through behind her, I could honestly say that she got what she deserved.

I immediately thought about the loss of my grandmother. This was the only way I knew I could get emotional. "Oh my God! When did this happen?" I asked.

The other detective cleared this throat and said, "We found her decomposed body in an abandoned building two and a half weeks ago, but we just found out a couple of days ago who she was. If it wasn't for her parents reporting her missing and then coming here to ID her body, we wouldn't have known who she was."

"What happened to her?"

"The forensic report states that she was shot in the head at close range."

"No, that can't be. Are you sure it's her?" I became panicked.

"Yes, we're sure it's her. We used her dental records to get a positive ID."

"Oh my God! Who could have done this to her?" I screamed.

"We were hoping you would be able to answer that question for us," the fat detective chimed in.

I sat there wearing an expression of despair. Tears fell from my eyes like a running faucet as both detectives examined my body language. About ten seconds later, I covered my entire face with both my hands while I cried uncontrollably. I knew I had to keep up this act. My freedom depended on it.

The fat detective handed me a couple of napkins to dry my tears. I took them and began to wipe my face. The moment I looked up at him, he threw another question at me.

"When was the last time you spoke to Nikki?"

I sat there and pondered for fear of fucking up and giving him the wrong answer. I didn't want it to seem like I was the last person that talked to her. So I thought carefully and then I said, "I'm not sure."

"Can you give me a more precise answer than that?"

"I don't remember. Shit, I've been away in Anguilla for a little over a month now."

"Well, did you speak with her while you were in Anguilla?"

"No."

"And why not?" His question cut like a sharp knife. "Were you two on speaking terms?"

"Of course we were," I snapped back.

"Well, if you two were on speaking terms, why hadn't you tried to contact her in almost a month?"

"I tried to call her, but she wouldn't answer her phone.

I figured she had fallen in love with a man and wanted to be left alone."

"That's bullshit, and you know it!" the fat detective roared. "I spoke with two women who used to work for you at your salon, and they told me a completely different story."

"Who?"

"Rachael and Carmen."

"I don't care what they told you. Everything that comes out of their mouths is nothing but lies."

"Well, they were both interviewed simultaneously by two different detectives, yet they still came up with the exact same story."

"And what story was that?" I asked, irritated.

"They both said you and Nikki hadn't been getting along for a while and that you kicked her out of the shop and your house a couple weeks before you left town."

"Rachael and Carmen said what?" I screamed with fury.

"Knock it off, Kira! And stop wasting our time. We know you know more than what you are telling us."

"I don't know shit!"

"Oh, you know something. Just like you knew about the drug dealings and the murders your ex-husband was involved in. Yeah, we know you talked yourself out of a federal prison sentence. Me and my partner got your entire file right here," he said, pointing down at a manila folder.

"OK. And so what? You would have done the same damn thing if you were facing fifteen years behind bars."

"But this is something different," the other detective said. "This was your blood relative. You and she came to Houston together to start a new life, so there was a strong bond there. Carmen said you two were really close until just recently."

"I don't give a fuck what Carmen said."

"Well, you better care about what I say," the fat detective said. "Because this is a much more serious matter than that federal case you were in involved in. I smell conspiracy to commit first-degree murder."

"That's bullshit! I didn't lay a fucking hand on her."

"Well, tell us who did. We know you know something."

"Are you fucking listening to me? I just told you I don't know shit."

"You can save that crap for a rookie. I'm a veteran in this game, and I feel it in my gut that you know more than what you are telling us. And when I find out that you do, I will personally make sure you won't see daylight until you are eighty."

"Am I under arrest right now?" I asked once again.

"No, you're not," the fat detective answered.

I stood. "Well, gentlemen, it was truly nice," I said with a half-smile.

Both detectives stood simultaneously, but the fat detective had more to say. "You know, once you walk out this door, you're on your own. There aren't going to be any plea bargains."

"What the fuck ever! Go beat the street and find the real killer!" I replied, and then I opened the door and slammed it as I exited the room.

It felt like a ton of bricks was lifted off my shoulders when the detectives allowed me to walk out of that room. But as soon as I turned the corner to enter the corridor that led to the main entrance, those same bricks were thrown back at me. Standing before me as if they were waiting for my arrival were my uncle and his wife, Nikki's parents.

My heart skipped a beat, but I kept my composure. Quickly, I slid off my engagement ring and dropped it into my pocket. I didn't want my uncle or his wife in my fucking business, questioning me about whether I was with another drug dealer.

Nikki's mother was the first to speak. This bitch hated my guts. It was even more evident when she spoke.

With watery eyes, she pointed her finger directly at me and gritted her teeth as she said, "I knew you were bad news from the day you were born! And now I see why your mother left you with your grandmother. You were like a bad seed, a black cloud looming over her head, so she had to get rid of your ass!"

"I beg your pardon?"

"You heard me!" she roared. "You are the reason my child is dead! If you would have left her alone, she would've graduated from Norfolk State and probably settled into a career. But, no! You had to drag her out here to this godforsaken place! It wouldn't surprise me if you encouraged her to hook up with another fucking drug dealer."

"Auntie, I didn't encourage Nikki to do anything," I replied, trying to sound as polite as possible.

Apparently not noticing my tone, she leaned forward and smacked the hell out of me. "Bitch, don't call me auntie! I will never be related to you. As far as I'm concerned, you are dead too."

I placed my hand on the side of my face to suppress the sting of her blow.

My uncle grabbed Auntie by her shoulders with both of his hands. "Calm down, honey, before you have another attack."

Totally ignoring him, she broke away from his grip and took two more steps toward me, her finger pointing directly at me. "You are going to get what's coming to you! Now you mark my words, sweetie! Your time is coming, and ain't nobody gonna be around to help you. Remember, everybody you used to deal with is dead! You are the only one left standing and breathing. Now I wonder why that is."

"Come on, honey, that's enough. We have to go!" my uncle told her.

"No, I'm not leaving until she tells me why everybody around her is dying."

I put my head down and walked away. She was on a rampage, and I wasn't about to let her make a spectacle of me, especially with all the cops hanging around. And now that I thought about it, it wouldn't surprise me if she was trying to set me up with all the fucking questions she was asking me. I was hip to her games. I wasn't that green. I had plenty of sense, whether or not she believed it.

I immediately exhaled when I exited the police precinct. With my carry-on bag and purse in hand, I walked straight down the boulevard, waiting for the next taxi to drive by so I could hop in. The sun was beaming down on me. It had to be every bit of one hundred degrees out here, and the humidity was even worse. At times, it felt like I couldn't breathe, but I kept walking.

In the distance, I heard my name called. I looked behind me and saw that it was my uncle running toward me. I stopped in my tracks and waited for him to approach me. Out of breath, he panted a little as he stopped before me. He immediately pressed his left hand against his chest.

"Are you all right?" I asked.

He nodded. "Yes, I'm fine. I just need to take a breather."

I grabbed him by his arm. "Take your time."

He took three deep breaths and then exhaled. "Look, I can't stay long. I just ran down here to apologize to you for the way my wife spoke to you."

"No, Uncle Lanier, you didn't have to do that."

"Listen, I know a lot of shit has happened, but I am not about to let that come between you and me. We are blood, and don't you ever forget that."

"I won't," I said, getting choked up.

He embraced me, so I hugged him back and wrapped my arms around him as tightly as I could. I realized at that point that he was the only living relative I had left. And to hear him tell me that he wouldn't let anyone come between us really made me feel some kind of way. I knew he had a genuine love for me, so that was all that mattered.

Right before he let me go, he looked into my eyes as if searching for something. It felt like he could see right through me. I felt very uneasy, so I put my head down.

He immediately grabbed me by the tip of my chin and lifted my head back up. "I'm going to ask you a question, and I want you to be honest with me, even if you think it will hurt me."

I developed a huge knot in my throat. From the look on my uncle's face, I could tell he was as serious as a fucking heart attack, and that he wanted me to ask me something to do with Nikki.

I took a deep breath. "OK." But on the inside, I was a nervous wreck. It felt like I was about to be interrogated all over again, but by a loved one this time. I gave him the most sincere expression I could muster, and then I gave him my undivided attention.

He took a deep breath. "Can you tell me anything about Nikki's murder? I mean, the police don't have any leads. And the motherfucker who did this to my baby has to pay for it. So if you know anything or anyone she was messing around with, please tell me."

"I'm sorry, Uncle Lanier, but I don't know anything. When Nikki and I got here, she and I didn't live together long. She and I got into a big argument, and shortly thereafter she moved out. She stopped working in my shop too, so we pretty much stopped all communication with each other."

"When was the last time you spoke to her?"

"About a month before I decided to leave the country."

"So she hadn't tried to contact you at all?"

"Nope."

"What about a man? Did you meet any of her male friends that might be linked to her murder?"

"She pretty much kept her personal life to herself. I used to try to get her to go out on double dates with me, but she would always refuse to go. I guess she was still bent out of shape behind that guy named Syncere she used to mess with back in Virginia."

Uncle Lanier shook his head in a frustrating manner. I could tell he wasn't pleased with what I had just said. He wanted something more solid, but I couldn't give it to him. I could see tears forming in his eyes, and my heart went out to him, but at the same time my hands were tied. I couldn't implicate myself just to make him feel better. Hell nah! I would be a damn fool. He was just gonna have to let the homicide detectives do their job, because I couldn't help him.

I rubbed him on his back and told him that everything was going to be all right, even though I knew it wouldn't. Bintu' and his family were notorious gangsters, and they were pros at organized crime, so there was no way the detectives or my uncle and his silly-ass wife would ever find out what went on in that abandoned warehouse. I made a vow to take what happened to my grave, and that was what I intended to do.

Uncle Lanier took another deep breath and then sighed heavily. "We are having Nikki's body shipped back to Virginia today because her funeral is this Friday at noon, which is three days from now. So please promise me that you'll come."

I hesitated before I answered, because the thought of going back to that place gave me the creeps. I had no life there. Everyone who was left living and breathing hated my fucking guts, so why even bother?

My uncle grabbed my hand. "Look, I know you have a lot of bad memories there. But could you at least block all of that out for this one day?"

My mind was telling me to tell my uncle, "Hell nah!" But my heart was forcing me to say the opposite. I went against my better judgment and told him, "I'm only doing this for you and Nikki."

He smiled. "That's all that matters." He kissed me on my forehead, said good-bye, and turned to leave.

I watched him as he made his way back toward the police precinct, his head held down the entire walk. It was evident that he was thinking about the loss of his only child. Nikki was his pride and joy. I knew her parents had many plans for her life. And now everything that they could have imagined would happen for her had gone up in smoke.

Although my uncle wouldn't admit it, I knew deep down inside that he blamed me for the day she dropped out of school, to the day she got arrested for transporting

Ricky's drugs, to the very day she got mixed up with that whack-ass nigga Syncere. No matter what I could have said, they would not have believed me if I told them that I had nothing to do with her getting with that guy. She'd met him on her own. But, hey, what could I say? You win some, and you lose some.

After my uncle disappeared behind the double doors of the police station, I turned around and started walking once again. My stroll only lasted ten seconds because a taxi rolled up quicker than I could blink.

I got into the air-conditioned cab with absolutely no idea where I wanted to go. I really didn't have a reason to be in Houston, other than to pay my real estate agent a fucking visit. How fucking grimy could she be, setting up my ass to be picked up?

I thought about calling her trashy ass and telling her I was taking my fucking house off the market and that I no longer need her damn assistance. But, nah, I was just gonna play her dumb ass at her own game and kill the bitch with kindness, see how she acted when she found out I wasn't behind bars.

I retrieved my BlackBerry from my handbag and dialed her office number. Her receptionist answered the line and connected me to her. "Hello, this is Kendra," she said.

"Hi, Kendra, this is Kira," I said, and then I fell silent.

"Oh, hey, girl. How-ow-ow you doing?" she stuttered.

"I'm doing fine. And you?"

"I'm g-g-g-good. How was your flight?"

"My flight was good. But are you sure you are all right?"

"Ahhh, yeah, I'm fine."

"So what time is the closing?" I asked, even though I knew there wasn't one.

"My assistant didn't call you?" Kendra asked, her voice barely audible.

"I didn't hear you, Kendra. Can you speak up?"

"My assistant was supposed to call you and tell you that the couple couldn't make the closing, so we're going to have to reschedule it for another day."

"When was I supposed to get this call?"

"She said she made the call yesterday."

"I'm sorry, but I didn't get that call, Kendra. And, anyway, I spoke to you yesterday morning to confirm the closing for today, and you told me everything was still a go."

"Yes, I did, and that was because everything was set in motion at that time. But right before I left the office yesterday I got the call from the couple's realtor saying that the couple hadn't come up with all the money they needed for their closing costs. So we had no choice but to reschedule."

"What's the couple's name?"

"I'm, well . . . I . . . um, don't have that information in front of me at the moment, but if you give me a second, I can have my assistant pull their folder," she replied, her voice fading in and out.

"That won't be necessary, Kendra. Just call me when you guys reschedule a closing date." It was pointless to continue probing her when all I was going to get was lies.

"Will do. But what are you going to do in the meantime?"

"I'm gonna go back to Anguilla."

"Well, you have a safe flight back."

"I will," I assured her, and then I hung up.

I called her so many bitches after I disconnected my line. She was a fucking fraud, and I wanted so badly to expose her ass. But I knew I had to wait for my day and time to do that. Right then, I needed the bitch to sell my house, and since she had an excellent track record of getting rid of properties, I decided to let her hold the ball.

Since my plans had changed and I was headed back out to Virginia, I knew I couldn't get back on a flight to go back to Anguilla. I instructed the driver to take me downtown to the Renaissance Hotel, which was one block over from where Fatu' had his penthouse.

After I checked into my room, I walked onto the balcony of my twentieth floor suite and gazed into the night. The streetlights were bright as hell, and the streets were busy as usual. I could see Fatu's old residence clear as day.

I stood there and thought back to the many nights I used to spend inside that building, and the mornings I used to wake up with breakfast served to me while still in bed. Not to mention the many times I sat up in his bed and wondered where he was.

I had to admit, life with him was an adventure. I just

couldn't believe how Nikki could go against me and sleep with him behind my back. Now, how scandalous was that? Did she hate me that much? Was I in any way toxic toward her? I mean, I couldn't imagine being so terrible to her that she would want to stab me in my back.

Then the way Fatu' carried me really had me taken aback. Who would have known? I was nothing but good to that son of a bitch, and look how he repaid me. He fucked my cousin and had her mind twisted the fuck up. I sure wished I could have gotten more out of him than I had, but it was too late now. He was gone, and so was she. So all that was left for me to do was move on and forget that they ever existed, which was what I planned to do.

I got undressed, took a quick shower, and ordered room service. I had no intention of leaving the hotel for fear that I'd run into someone I didn't want to see. I had a juicy filet mignon with a baked potato and a side of steamed broccoli. After that hearty meal, I settled down and watched an old western movie with Clint Eastwood. Shortly thereafter I dozed off.

The next morning I got up and got dressed. I had no plans to stick around in Houston, so I got a taxi driver to take me back to the airport. The quicker I got out of Houston, the better. When I got to the airport, I went to the reservation desk and bought myself a round-trip ticket to Virginia.

The next flight leaving was in two hours, so I had a little bit of time to mess around. Since I hadn't had any time to get a bite to eat while I was at the hotel, I sat down at one of the cafés in the airport and ordered a breakfast platter with three strips of bacon, two scrambled eggs, hash browns, and two pieces of toast. The eggs looked really wet and uncooked, so I devoured the bacon and the toast and finished off my meal with a tall cup of apple juice.

Later as I waited for my flight, I got a call from Kendra. I answered after the second ring. "Hello," I said.

"Hi, Kira. This is Kendra."

"How can I help you, Kendra?"

She sighed heavily. "Kira, I have a confession to make. I tossed and turned all last night thinking about you."

"What about?" I asked, even though I knew what she was hinting at.

"I haven't been totally honest with you about why I needed you to come back to Houston. See, I got a call from a Houston homicide detective wanting to know your whereabouts. He said he was investigating a murder and you could probably help him. So I asked him what he needed from me, and that was when he told me to call you with some bogus story about me having a seller for your house so you would come back to the States. Now, believe me, I was reluctant to help him at first, but when I sat back and thought about it, I remembered back when my sister was murdered while some crazy guys were doing a drive-by, and no one ever came forward to give information so those guys could pay for what they did. So, you see, I felt compelled to help him. I couldn't see doing it any other way."

"Look, Kendra, you don't have to go through that whole spiel. I understand."

"No, you don't, Kira. This was something I had to do for my sister, so it had nothing to do with you as a person."

"If it's any consolation, Kendra, I'm OK with what you did. I mean, it would've happened sooner or later."

"So you forgive me?"

"You are a'ight. Everything is cool."

"So when are you leaving to go back to Anguilla?"

"In a few days. I've got to head back to my hometown to tie up a few loose ends."

"When are you leaving?"

"Today. I'm at the airport as we speak."

"Well, you have a safe flight and make sure you call me before you head back to Anguilla."

"Will do," I said and then hung up.

SAYING GOOD-BYE

When my plane arrived in Norfolk, I walked straight into the terminal with my heart beating rapidly. I was afraid that either the feds were hiding out somewhere in the airport waiting patiently to take me into custody for something really bogus, or Ricky's people were disguised and just looking for the right opportunity to put a bullet in my head. I knew I would feel this way when I touched down in this city. It never failed.

I remember the day I came out of Witness Protection. I was a complete basket case. Always looking over my shoulders, wondering who was watching me. I hated feeling that way. I mean, who wanted to carry that uneasy feeling with them every single day? Not me. I couldn't do it. Which was why I got the hell out of Virginia. The quicker I paid my respects to Nikki, the faster I could get the hell out of here again.

Doing what I did best, I hopped into a taxi and instructed the driver to take me to the Hilton, which was right on the corner of Military Highway and North Hampton Boulevard, only five minutes from the airport. This was a prime location for me. I knew no one I knew would hang out there, because it was more upscale than most hotels in the city. A lot of pilots, flight attendants, and business executives frequented this place. The hustlers I knew were more likely to get a room in downtown Norfolk at the Sheraton or the Marriott. And when they wanted to be incognito to creep with one of their side hoes, they'd take a trip up to Williamsburg or Lightfoot and get a room out there. I knew their fucking tricks. That was how I always stayed a few steps ahead of them.

Speaking of which, that was what I should have told Nikki's mother when the bitch asked me why I was still alive while everybody else kept falling down around me like flies. Shit, if you asked me, they were all just dealt a fucked-up hand. I couldn't explain it any better than that. But the next time she came out her mouth and insinuated that I was the reason Nikki was murdered, I would tell her just that. Fuck it! I was so tired of biting my tongue and being the nice guy. From here on out, everyone would feel my wrath. That was my word.

Driving at the speed of twenty miles per hour, the taxi driver finally got me to my destination fifteen minutes later, although it should have only taken five minutes. I was annoyed, but I didn't take out my frustrations on him. I paid him while the bellman opened the door to the cab.

After I got out of the cab, I handed the bellman a crisp ten-dollar bill and headed straight into the hotel lobby, which was somewhat empty. It was probably because it was a Thursday, and tourists normally started their vacations on a Friday. Once my room was paid for, I got on the elevator and made my way up to the fifth floor.

Inside my room, the curtains were drawn back, allowing the sun to beam right in. I dropped my handbag and my carry-on on top of the bed, kicked off my sneakers, and sat down.

I gazed outside and wondered what was going on out there in those streets, since Ricky, Russell, Brian, and the rest of the crew were no longer out there to throw their weight around, I knew there had to be a new crew out there holding down the streets. That was just how the game was played. When one crew left the set, another one came right in and set up shop. It was called free rein, the last rule in the hustler's manual. Every cat knew that.

As I thought about the rough streets of Norfolk, I couldn't help but think back on the things I did when I'd lived here, and how popular I was.

Niggas loved me, and the bitches hated my guts. I was hated by some of the hottest chicks out here. But what they didn't have that I did have was Ricky, a hot commodity when he was alive. I literally had to fight a few hoes to keep them in check. The street chicks from VA ain't to be fucked with. They would fuck your man right in front of you. Oh, yeah, most of them were scandalous, so I kept a blade on me at all times. Being back in Virginia really had me remembering how my life used to be. They were not pleasant memories.

After I finished reminiscing, I ordered some room service and chilled in the room for the rest of the evening. Right after I set my empty dishes outside the room, I climbed into bed and dialed my baby's number.

He answered after the second ring. "I was wondering when you were going to call," he said.

The very next morning I got up, called Donovan to let him know that I was about to hop in the shower, and told him that I would call him back as soon as I left the funeral. He said, "OK," and then we hung up.

The hot water in the shower did me some justice. I didn't want to get out, but I knew I had somewhere to be. I got dressed in a black one-shoulder dress I had stuffed away in my carry-on bag, and then I slipped on my shoes and grabbed my handbag.

Before I left my room, I looked down at my engagement ring and, once again, decided not to wear it to the funeral.

The funeral started at noon, and I wanted to be on time, so instead of taking another taxi, I called Enterprise to rent a car, and had them pick me up. I needed a car to get around anyway, since I wanted to do a little sightseeing before I left, and it would have been extremely expensive to do it while the meter was running. It didn't take long for me to get the car, so I was on the road and within two miles of the church in less than thirty minutes.

When I arrived at the church on the corner of Princess Anne Road and Church Street, I took a deep breath and convinced myself that I would be all right. Cars and trucks were parked everywhere. I had no idea

Nikki's funeral would be that damn big. The church was packed from one wall to the other. When I looked at the faces of all those people I realized that they were relatives of hers from her mother's side of the family. There were also a lot of chicks who went to Norfolk State with her sitting near her relatives too. I smiled and took a seat in the third row.

Uncle Lanier and his wife were seated in the very first row. I wanted to be as far away from them as possible. I couldn't afford to be humiliated in front of everyone—not today, or any other day for that matter.

Finally, after everyone got to their seats, the minister started the service. Nikki's mother immediately broke down into tears and cried the entire time. During the eulogy I heard Nikki's aunt on her mother's side say that Nikki was in a better place.

I immediately thought about the day Nikki was murdered. I didn't remember her asking God for forgiveness. She was pleading for her life as I recalled. I don't think she had enough time to talk to God. If she did, she must've snuck in a quick forgive-me prayer underneath her breath right before that iron went right through her. For her sake, I sure hope she did. From the way my grandmother used to talk about how hot hell was, I wouldn't want to wish that on my worst enemy. Oh, well, only God know where she would end up.

Immediately after the eulogy was read, some godforsaken old lady got up to sing "His Eye is on the Sparrow," and I swear to you, I wanted to puke. This lady sounded like pure shit, and I wanted so badly to tell her to shut up, while everyone around me was telling her to take her time.

Aside from that, this was truly a sad occasion. I could now imagine how my funeral was when everyone thought I was dead and I was hiding out in the Witness Protection Program. To see someone you were once close to go away from this earth was like losing a part of yourself. And even though Nikki and I weren't on the best of terms before she got murdered, in some kind of weird way, I felt a sense of loss. I wasn't that fucking coldhearted, at least not to my family.

After the burial everybody got in their cars and followed one another back to my uncle's home for a gathering. I started not to go, but my uncle insisted that I needed to be amongst family, so I tagged along. When I arrived at his home, I did everything within my power to avoid a run-in with his wife, who hated my guts. Whenever I saw her coming in my direction, I went the opposite way.

I greeted a few people who knew me through Nikki. They all spoke very highly of her, talking about how she was gonna be missed because she had been an instrumental part in their lives. I found that very hard to believe, because she was a jealous bitch to me. She tried everything in her power to destroy me, so I wouldn't be missing her at all. I honestly wanted to throw up when I heard one of her old classmates say how Nikki used to have her back and how she would take her home on the nights they had late classes together.

"I will never forget her," the chick said.

I looked at her and wanted to throw up. They didn't know Nikki like I knew her. She had them fooled. And I refused to listen to any more of their dramatic stories.

I looked for the nearest exit and made my way toward it. When I entered the hallway that led to the foyer, I heard voices. One of the voices belonged to Uncle Lanier, but I couldn't identify the other voice. It bothered me that I couldn't place the voice, so I made it my business to quench my curiosity.

As I approached my uncle and the other mystery man, I overheard my uncle say, "I want to do it myself, but I just don't have the guts to do it."

The two men were only a few feet away from me. All I had to do was walk two more feet and turn a corner to come into the foyer. As soon as I did that, I was in full view. I was blown away when I saw my uncle talking to Tony, the baby daddy of my late friend and business partner, Rhonda.

The last time I had seen Tony was right before I got shot and went into Witness Protection, so I really didn't know whether to give him my condolences concerning Rhonda, or just hug him. I was totally speechless, but something inside me got up the urge to do the first thing that came to mind. I finally smiled and said, "Well, hello."

Tony smiled back at me. "And hello to you too," he said, and then he reached out and gave me a hug.

After we embraced, I felt a sense of warmth. All the guilt I felt at not attending Rhonda's funeral or paying him a visit to check up on the kids went right out the window. "What a surprise to see you here. I didn't know you knew my uncle," I commented, looking at him and my uncle.

My uncle spoke up first. "I never told you I met him?"

"Not that I remember."

"It must've slipped my mind. But I've known Tony for years. He used to work for me some years back while I was a supervisor in Wal-Mart's warehouse."

Tony laughed. "Yeah, but tell her how long I kept that job."

My uncle laughed. "He didn't stay with us long. I was actually off the day he got fired by the other supervisor, so we didn't get to see each other before he left. But it's funny how life is. Because the day I went by your shop to check on Nikki, he was dropping off his girlfriend Rhonda, and we recognized each other that very second."

"Where was I?" Before I realized what I had said, it was too late to retract my question. I looked at my uncle oddly and hoped he would be clever enough not to reveal my whereabouts to Tony.

"That happened during the time you went away. Nikki and Rhonda were handling the shop for you."

I was truly relieved at the way my uncle handled his response. "So what are you two talking about?"

"We were just talking about the loss of Nikki and Rhonda."

"Yeah, it's a tragic thing." I sighed. "It feels like I lost two sisters."

"Yeah, I'm sure."

Tony didn't utter a word.

"So, where are the kids?" I asked him, changing the subject.

"At the house with a friend of mine."

"Well, would it be all right if I saw them before I got back on my flight and headed out of here?"

"When are you leaving?"

"In the morning."

"So soon?"

"Yeah, I got to get out of here. There's nothing going on around here that I need to be a part of. And, besides, I have a man back home who's waiting patiently for me to get back there."

Tony and my uncle both smiled.

"Where are you staying tonight?" Tony asked.

"At the Hilton on Military Highway."

"Are you getting ready to head there now?"

"I was. Why?"

"Well, if you'd like, you can follow me back to my spot and see the kids before you head back to your hotel."

"OK. Sounds good. I can do that."

"All right then, let's go." Tony turned toward my uncle and gave him a handshake. "Holla at me later," he told him.

"I will," my uncle replied, and then he escorted me and Tony to the front door.

Before I walked out of the house, I gave Uncle Lanier a big hug and told him I loved him. He expressed his love for me as well and then told me to call him before I left town. I assured him that I would.

When Tony and I got outside, I got into my rental car and started my ignition. Meanwhile Tony got into a sky-blue Toyota Camry that once belonged to Rhonda. I remembered when she'd first bought that car. She was so excited to get something brand-new. She knew she couldn't afford the type of vehicle I drove, so she got the next best thing. Plus, it was more pleasing to her pockets. I was so happy for her that day. I just wished she was here today to drive that bad boy, because I knew that she would've taken good care of it.

Tony started his ignition and signaled for me to follow him, so I did just that.

BEHIND DOOR #1

The ride to Tony's place didn't take long at all. When we jumped on Highway 264, I thought we were headed out to Stony Point, located off Newtown Road in Norfolk. But when we didn't get off at the Newtown Road exit, I figured he'd moved out of that neighborhood and taken his kids somewhere else. I ended up following him to South Military Highway to an apartment complex called Dockside.

As we pulled into the parking lot, I felt a sense of guilt about seeing Rhonda's children, because they no longer had their mother around. But I also felt love filling my heart because I was about to see the children after all this time. When I got out of the car, I took a deep breath and followed Tony to the front door.

Surprisingly, Tony's friend opened the front door before he could unlock it. She stood there in the doorway wearing the evilest stare.

I smiled. "Hello."

She ignored me and looked directly at Tony. "Who is this?"

While Tony explained to her silly ass who I was, I stood there with my expensive handbag clutched tightly in my hands, making sure she could see it was high-end. I even stuck out my right leg so she could see that my Marc Jacobs shoes. I knew she couldn't afford the attire I was used to wearing, so I made her grit on me even more when I sighed heavily like my time was being wasted.

"Am I going to see the kids or not?" I asked. "Because if I'm intruding on her time and space, then I can take my ass to the mall and do a little shopping before I leave town," I said to Tony. I looked back at the chick to see her reaction.

"Well, carry your ass then!" she roared.

I smiled. "Sweetie, you don't even know me to be popping shit like this!"

"Trust me, I can do and say what the fuck I want to."

I looked back at Tony. "Can you please handle her before—"

"Before you do what?" She took two steps toward me. This chick was so close to me, she could've grabbed me around my throat with ease.

Luckily, Tony got between us. "Shannon, go 'head with that crazy-ass shit! All Kira came here to do is see the kids, and then she's bouncing."

"That bitch ain't coming in here!"

"I ain't gotta come in there!"

Tony pushed Shannon backward. "Get cha ass back in the house. I ain't got time for this bullshit. This girl ain't did shit to you for you to be acting like this."

"I'm just tired of you bringing a whole bunch of bitches to this house. Last week, it was that chick named

Sheila, and come to find out, you were fucking her. So, for all I know, she could be another one of the bitches you be fucking behind my back."

Tony screamed, "I ain't trying to hear that shit, so shut the fuck up!"

Shannon stormed back in the house. She went straight to the hall closet by the front door, reached inside, grabbed her coat and purse, and then stormed right back out past us. I turned to see where she was going. When I saw her hop into a green Nissan Sentra, I wondered why she carried on the way she did.

A brown-skinned chick about two inches taller than me, Shannon was a very pretty young lady. Her hair, styled in a silk wrap, was very long, and she had it cut in layers. But I could tell it was a weave. She looked like the actress Gabrielle Union, but her weight was a little more on the thick side. Her taste in designers wasn't high-end, because the jean shorts, spaghetti-strap top, and three-inch slingback sandals she wore couldn't come from anywhere else except bottom-dollar stores. Her whole ensemble looked cheap, so I knew she got a fever when she first looked at me and saw I was rocking an all-black Burberry one-shoulder dress with a black Chanel purse.

When she drove off, she pressed down on the accelerator, squealing her tires like she was a fucking racecar driver. I laughed underneath my breath because she looked really ridiculous in that little tin can car.

I turned my attention back to Tony. I smiled and said, "I see you got yourself a new wifey!"

"Nah, Shannon's just my friend. I ain't ready to get into another serious relationship. I got too much shit on my plate right now to be dealing with emotional attachments."

I sighed. "Well, emotional baggage is definitely what women bring to the table."

He nodded. "True. True."

"How do you think the kids are going to react when they see me?" I asked as we entered his apartment.

"I'm not sure, but we're about to find out." Tony started yelling their names. When they didn't answer, he said, "They probably can't hear me because they got that TV up really loud."

As I stepped into the hallway, I stood there alongside the wall and waited for him to close the door behind us so he could escort me to where the children were.

But before we could move one step, both kids came rushing down the hallway toward me. "Auntie Kira," they both yelled.

My heart instantly filled with joy when I saw Li'l Tony and Meagan coming toward me. I bent down and extended both of my arms. They rushed to me and fell into my arms.

"Where you been at?" Rhonda's nine-year-old son asked.

"Yeah, Auntie Kira, where you been? We missed you," seven-year-old Meagan said.

I looked at them both. "I missed y'all too, but I had to leave town for a while."

"Why?" Meagan wanted to know.

"Because something came up and I had to hurry up and leave."

"You know my mommy died, right?" Li'l Tony asked.

Shocked by his candor, I looked up at Tony to see his reaction, and also to see if he would answer the question for me, because I really didn't know what to say. Yes, I knew Rhonda got killed, but how would I explain to a child that I knew about his mother's death, but didn't go to her funeral, or even check on them to see how they were doing? I'd totally deserted them. And I was feeling the guilt rise up within me.

Since Tony didn't come to my rescue, I exhaled and said, "Yes, sweetie, I know."

"Our daddy said she's in heaven with God," Meagan said.

"Your daddy is right."

"Our daddy also said that it was you and Nikki's fault that my mommy got killed."

Without warning, Tony smacked his son on the back of his head.

"Owwwwww!" Li'l Tony grabbed the back of his head.

"It's gonna hurt worse than that if you keep running your mouth. You don't know what you're talking about."

Taken aback by Li'l Tony's comment, I was speechless. I honestly didn't know what else to say. At that very moment I wanted to shrink to the size of a mouse and crawl right into a hole. And since I knew I wouldn't be able to pull that one off, I looked back at Tony and smiled gracefully. I tried to block out everything around me for just one second, but it didn't work, so I looked back into Li'l Tony's eyes and said, "No, sweetie! I didn't have anything to do with what happened to your mother. Now I can't speak for Nikki, but I can definitely speak for myself. And I will tell you this. If I was around, I would've made sure nothing happened to your mother," I said, using my peripheral vision to look at Tony. I wanted to see his expression, but he must've known I was watching him, because he didn't flinch.

Tony then grabbed Li'l Tony by the back of his shirt and began pulling him down the hallway. "Bring your big mouth on down here to the living room and have a damn seat before I tear up your ass!" Tony escorted his son toward the living room area of the house.

As Meagan followed behind them, I followed behind her. What I really wanted to do was turn around and go right back through the door I'd just come through. I honestly didn't want to believe that Tony blamed me for Rhonda's murder. In fact, he didn't give me that impression when I'd first approached him at my uncle's house.

When I got to the living room, Tony asked me if I wanted something to drink, but I turned him down. I took a seat beside the kids on the sofa to watch TV. I draped my handbag over my lap and sat there like I was really into the show the children were watching.

"Can I use the bathroom?" I asked.

Tony took a seat on the lounge chair. "Yeah, go ahead. It's that door underneath the stairwell."

"Thanks."

I got up from the chair and raced to the hallway bathroom. As soon as I closed the door behind me, I sat on the side of the bathtub and exhaled. A ton of things ran through my mind at once. I tried to collect my thoughts, but I couldn't.

Under normal circumstances, I would have stepped to Tony and addressed the situation, but for some reason, I felt out of sync with him. I was never his best friend, but we were really cool when Rhonda was alive. I remember him asking me to babysit the kids on a couple of occasions so he and Rhonda could either go out or stay in and have time alone. Every time he needed me to come through for him, I did, so it really was a shocker to me that he was holding back his true feelings and wasn't being straight up with me. I guess I was gonna have to approach him with it. He and I had come too far to let something as serious as this come between us.

I stood and looked into the bathroom mirror. "OK, Kira, you can do it, girl," I said to myself. Before I walked out of the bathroom, I pushed down the handle on the toilet to make it seem like I had just used it, and then I turned on the bathroom faucet and pretended like I was washing my hands. As I prepared to exit the bathroom, I took another deep breath, exhaled, and strolled back into the living room, where Tony and the kids were watching TV.

As soon as I walked into the room, I noticed that Tony was gone. The children were still seated in the same places on the sofa. I asked Li'l Tony where his father was.

"I think he went into the kitchen," he said.

Badly wanting to set the record straight with Tony, I backed up into the hallway and turned around to see if he was in fact in the kitchen. I walked the short distance to the kitchen and made a left turn around the corner. To my surprise, Tony wasn't in the kitchen. I started to call out his name, but I figured that wherever he was, he'd be right back. This apartment only had two levels, so he was probably on the second floor.

I turned to go back into the living room, but the sound of Tony's voice stopped me in my tracks. I paused for a minute to hear from which direction his voice was coming. It sounded like he was engaged in a conversation.

I immediately turned around toward the front door and stood still. His words became clearer as I got closer. Then I heard him say, "I can handle that. That ain't no problem."

I took two more steps toward the front door so I could reach over and grab the handle to twist it and open the door.

"OK, I'll do it, but he better have my money in hand when I get there," Tony said.

Before he could say another word, I opened the front door. He looked at me like I was a fucking ghost. "Are you all right?" I asked him.

Instead of responding to my question, he spoke into the receiver of his cell phone. "Eh, yo, homeboy, let me call you back in a few minutes." Then he shoved his phone into his pants pocket.

"I'm sorry. Did I scare you?"

"Nah, you a'ight."

"Well, the reason I came looking for you is because I wanted to talk to you while the kids weren't around."

"What's up?"

"Can we talk out here?"

"Yeah, but close the door behind you."

I closed the door and stepped onto the front porch. Standing only a foot away from me, Tony gave me his undivided attention. I cleared my throat and said, "Look, Tony, I've known you for about the same amount of time as I knew Rhonda. I've always treated you and Rhonda like family. Now I know that it's been a while since I've been around, especially since I'm the godmother of those kids in there, but as long as I stand here breathing, I would never do anything, nor have I ever done anything to put you, those kids, or Rhonda in a predicament that would harm any of you. Now I know Rhonda is gone and we can't bring her back, but I swear to you that it wasn't my fault she got killed."

Tony smiled. "I can't believe you believed what Li'l Tony said. Kira, I don't blame you for Rhonda's murder."

"But why would he make that type of comment?" I asked. His words had really hurt me.

"He must've heard bits and pieces of my conversation with Shannon and got all mixed up. I mean, that's the only way I can see it. But you really shouldn't let what he said bother you, because I don't feel that way about you at all."

Tony seemed sincere in what he was saying was, so I

let what Li'l Tony said to me ride. I was glad I got that shit off my chest, so now I could move forward.

As Tony and I continued to converse, Meagan opened the front door. "Daddy, Li'l Tony turned the TV channel while I was watching *Hannah Montana*."

"Tell 'im I said he better turn the channel back or I'm gon' beat his ass!"

"OK." Meagan dashed back into the house.

About five seconds later she came running back outside. "Daddy, every time I turn it to channel twenty-nine, he turns the TV back to what he wants to watch."

Tony asked me to excuse him and then stormed into the house. Meagan and I followed. He chastised him, and the kids finally calmed down.

A few minutes later Tony told Meagan and Li'l Tony to get ready so they could leave to go over to their grandmother's house.

"Are you talking about Rhonda's mom?" I asked.

"Yes. I told her I would bring the kids over for a visit today."

"How is she doing?"

"She's fine. Wanna ride over there with us?"

"How long do you plan to be there?"

"Not long. I'm really just gonna drop off the kids."

"I don't wanna go over Grandma's house," Li'l Tony said. "I wanna stay here."

"Me either, Daddy. I wanna stay here with you."

"Well, I ain't gon' be here. I got to go out for a while."

"Well, can we go with you?" Meagan asked.

"No, you can't."

"I don't wanna go with you. I just want to stay home so I can play with my Xbox game."

"Well, that's not happening. Both of y'all are going to your grandmother's house, and that's it. Now get ready because we're leaving in five minutes."

Li'l Tony and Meagan both dragged themselves out of the living room and headed upstairs to their rooms to get what they were going to need while at their grandmother's house.

I stood there in amazement. I wanted to applaud Tony for acting as mother and father since Rhonda's passing, for his efforts to keep his family together. But then I figured he knew he had done something right, because his children definitely listened to him.

A few minutes later everyone stood in a huddle at the front door, ready to leave. I stood among them, not knowing whether I would leave with them or head back to my hotel.

Tony asked, "So are you hanging out with us or going elsewhere?"

I thought for a second. "I guess I can hang out with y'all for a few, since I didn't have any other plans."

Meagan jumped for joy, while Li'l Tony just stood there with no expression at all. I figured he couldn't care less either way. Tony, on the other hand, smiled.

After we all climbed into the car, Tony started the ignition and then he drove off to connect to the main road. The ride back down South Military Highway toward

Highway 264 was very peaceful.

Tony had Jay-Z's latest CD playing. Everyone was quiet during the ride, except Li'l Tony, who sung every word on every Jay-Z track.

I laughed. He reminded me of how I used to be as a child. I was a music fanatic. I knew every word of any song that came on the radio. I got that from my mother, who had a huge album collection that included geniuses like Gladys Knight, Diana Ross, The Temptations, and Earth, Wind & Fire. While my mother played her music, I used to sit back in the den and learn the words to those songs like I was going to get quizzed on them, though I couldn't carry a note from one room to the next.

I put my head back against the headrest and closed my eyes, thinking about my mother.

"Are you all right?" Tony asked me.

Without opening my eyes, I assured him I was fine.

"Is the music too loud?"

"No, it's OK."

"Are you sure? Because I can turn it down if it's too loud."

I opened my eyes and looked directly at him. "Trust me, I am fine," I told him and then I laid my head back and closed my eyes again.

About ten minutes into the drive, Tony's cell phone rang. He allowed it to ring about five times before he answered. It annoyed the hell out of me that he'd let it ring so long. I opened my eyes to see what the problem was.

"Hello," he finally said.

I couldn't hear the caller, but from the look on Tony's face, I could tell that the caller was just as annoyed as I was.

"Nah, nigga, it can't be like that. I got my shorties with me." Tony paused.

"Yo, we gon' have to set up something for later, because I can't get into that right now," he said and then he paused once more.

"A'ight, later." Tony ended his call.

Now I know I am not an expert of any kind, but from the sound of that conversation I could only assume that Tony was talking about drugs. Ever since I'd known him, he had always tried to get a decent cocaine hookup. He'd always wanted to play with the big dogs, handle large sums of cash, and drive the expensive whips, but no one in the game wanted to fuck with him.

Your average wannabe nigga, Tony couldn't flip a bird if his life depended on it. He hustled backward. Rhonda used to say he would be gone all day long, and wouldn't have shit to show for it. She couldn't figure out how he used to have so much dope but never made a decent profit out of it. Now I saw him going around that same mountain. He hadn't learned shit. And from the looks of it, he probably never would.

We finally arrived at Rhonda's mother's house in Coleman Place, a very quiet area of Norfolk. From what I'd heard, Ms. Mavis had lived in this house since Rhonda was a little girl.

She met us on her front porch and greeted us with a big smile. "Y'all better get on in this house and stop walking like you got molasses in your butts."

I smiled and put a little more speed in my step.

Ms. Mavis was a beautiful lady. She had dark skin with beautiful hazel brown eyes. Her hair was long, but she kept it back in a ponytail. She was average height and very curvy. She reminded me of Phylicia Rashad from *The Cosby Show*.

As I reached her side, she embraced me with every muscle in her body. She definitely made me feel loved. "What a pleasant surprise!" she said. Then she smacked Tony on the arm. "Why didn't you tell me you were bringing Kira over here?"

"Trust me, it was a last-minute decision."

I chuckled. "It's not his fault, Ms. Mavis. I just decided to tag along, since I didn't have anything else to do."

"What's going on with you? Are you moving back home?"

I sighed heavily. "No, ma'am! I wouldn't move back to VA if somebody paid me and built me a home from the ground up."

"Come on now. You know you miss living here," Ms. Mavis joked.

"The only thing I miss is you and these kids. All that other mess, I can't be bothered with."

"Well, you're gonna be bothered today, 'cause I got a pot of hot chicken soup on the stove right now. So y'all come on in here and get you a bowl," Ms. Mavis said as she led the way inside.

It had been a little over a year since I'd been in Ms. Mavis's house. The last time I was there I had come to pay my respects for Rhonda's death. I had left her a nice piece of change too. I wondered if she'd used any of it for Rhonda's kids, since that was the reason I left it.

She gave me a brief tour of her living room, showing me all of the pictures Rhonda took through the years, while Tony and the kids raced for the kitchen.

As I looked at each framed picture, Ms. Mavis had a story to tell.

But one particular picture stood out. A photo of me, my late husband Ricky, Rhonda, and my old stylist, Sunshine, at the grand opening of my hair salon. We were dressed to kill. And we looked so damn happy. Ricky stood in the middle, between me and that bitch Sunshine. Looking at him now with his arm around her waist, I should've known he was fucking her behind my back. Scandalous motherfuckers! Yeah, they deserved each other!

On the other hand, Rhonda sure didn't deserve to get killed. I just hoped that I could convey that in a suitable manner and leave in good graces with both Tony and Ms. Mavis before I headed back out of town.

Tony and both of his children were in the kitchen digging deep inside their bowls of soup. Ms. Mavis offered me some, but I declined. I lied to her and told her that I'd gotten a bite to eat right before I'd arrived at Tony's place.

So Ms. Mavis and I ended up taking a seat in the den area, where we chatted a little bit about what my life had been like since leaving Virginia. I painted a beautiful picture of me settling down with Mr. Right and having a successful hair salon and day spa back in Houston. I even lied to her and told her that I might be expecting a baby, and she seemed very happy for me.

We even reminisced about Rhonda helping me run the business and being such a great mother.

Tony walked in the room when I was telling a story about how Rhonda had once handled an irate customer for me. I couldn't tell you what his problem was, but he abruptly cut me off in mid-sentence, telling me, he was ready to go.

Ms. Mavis wasn't ready for me to leave and wanted me to finish the story.

"Ms. Mavis, I just got a call and I got to go," he informed her.

"Why don't you just leave and come back to get her later?" Ms. Mavis asked.

"I can't, because I'm not coming back this way."

"It's OK, Ms. Mavis. I can call you later and tell you the story some other time." I stood and gave her a big hug and kissed her on her cheek. "You take care of my godchildren."

She smiled and held me tightly. "Oh, you can bet your last dollar I will do just that!"

While she walked me to the front door, I slid her my new cell number and told her never to hesitate to call me. She assured me that she would. I hugged her once more, and then I made my exit to meet Tony, who had already gone outside.

BEHIND DOOR #2

When I got into the car with Tony, he was on the phone, but he quickly got off. "I gotta make one quick stop before I go back to my house," he told me.

"That's cool."

Tony pulled away from Ms. Mavis's house while she stood there on the front porch and waved good-bye. Once she was out of sight, I turned my attention to him. "Where you got to go that's so important?" I wanted to know.

"Well, I've got to stop and get some gas first. And then I've got to meet up with my homeboy before he leaves to go out of town."

"Hold, you! Meeting your homeboy before he goes out of town sure sounds like a drug buy." I chuckled, but I was serious as a fucking heart attack. Shit, I didn't come all the way back to Virginia to be getting arrested on a bogus-ass drug charge behind some wannabe-ass hustler. I had too much at stake, and my freedom was at the top of the list.

"Come on, Kira. What kind of nigga you think I am? I don't get down like that," he said as he pulled into a Shell gas station.

When Tony got out the car to go pay for the gas, I

told him I was going to Feather-N-Fin to get a sweet tea. I strutted myself across the street, and when I got to the door, this older gentleman held it open for me. After I stepped inside the restaurant, I thanked him.

It was a little after four in the evening, so I knew there would be a crowd of people trying to get their eat on. I got in line and waited my turn. The line was moving pretty quickly, so I knew I would be in and out of there before Tony finished pumping his gas.

"Can I take your order?" the young lady asked me. She was a pretty young girl with blonde micro braids. She looked like she was every bit of eighteen or nineteen years old.

After I told her I wanted a medium sweet iced tea, she rang it up. I handed her my debit card, but she told me there was a five-dollar minimum purchase requirement to use my card. Since I didn't have any money on me and I wanted my tea, I ordered a boneless chicken breast sandwich with cheese.

Once she added my sandwich to the order, she swiped my card, but for some reason, my card wouldn't process. The screen on the terminal displayed the words COMM ERROR, meaning, there was a bad connection with the phone line.

"Why don't you disconnect your phone line and plug it back," I suggested. "That always worked for me when I had a merchant machine at my hair salon."

"You do hair?" the young girl asked as she unhooked the phone cord from the terminal and then plugged it back in.

"I used to."

"Where did you do hair at?" she asked, waiting for the machine to crank back up.

"I owned a shop on Newtown Road called Millennium Styles, but then I closed it and moved out of town."

"Wait a minute! I thought I remembered you!"

Shocked that she knew me, I stood there and waited for her to jog my memory.

"My sister Sunshine used to do hair there," she said. "Remember the time I came up there and brought her some balloons and a card on her birthday and she got all happy? But when she opened her card and realized I hadn't put any money inside, she started complaining, and that was when you took up for me and told her to be grateful."

Looking at the young girl again, I felt like I was looking at Sunshine. In fact, she looked like Sunshine's twin. I assumed she knew nothing about the affair that Sunshine had with my late husband, since she seemed excited to see me. This young girl made me feel like I was an old friend.

"What was your name again?" I asked her.

"Fionna. But my friends call me Fifi." She smiled.

I smiled back and thought about how she seemed to be in great spirits for someone who had lost her sister. I wondered if Sunshine ever spoke about me in a bad way. Well, if she did, this chick who stood in front of me truly knew how to mask her real feelings. "Well, Fifi," I said, "I am truly sorry about your loss."

"Oh, you don't have to feel sorry. She's in a better

place. And, besides, you should be happy that she's gone, considering all the drama she took you through."

"What kind of drama would that be?" I asked, even though I knew what Fionna was referring to.

"All I'm saying is that I should be the one apologizing to you, since it was my sister who tore your marriage apart by sleeping with Ricky behind your back."

Once again shocked by her comment, I stood there motionless. I didn't know whether to start cursing or break down in tears. Here I was again reminded about something that happened in my past. I didn't need that in my life, especially since I was trying to move on. Ricky and Sunshine were both distant memories, and I believed they'd gotten what they deserved. So if their souls were in hell, that was where they were meant to be.

I had to take a deep breath and exhale before I could make a rebuttal. After I got myself together, I asked Fionna how long she'd known about their relationship.

"I'm not sure. But I do remember when he stopped over her apartment to drop off some money. It was a Sunday night, because I was in the living room watching *The Wire* on HBO. She took him into her bedroom hoping I couldn't hear their conversation, but I heard every word they said anyway, especially the part about the baby."

"What baby?"

"I don't know if she was pregnant for real, but I did hear her telling him that she needed some abortion money because she wasn't ready to have a baby."

"Wow! You have got to be kidding me," I said, heartbroken.

"Nah, I'm dead serious!"

Now I knew Ricky slept around on me, and I knew he had an affair with Sunshine, but to later find out that she could have possibly carried his baby was a huge slap in the face. Ricky really didn't give a fuck about me! He fucked all his side chicks without a stitch of protection, so I wouldn't be surprised if that nigga had at least a dozen kids running around between Virginia and D.C. The thought of all the times he betrayed gave me an instant headache, so I tried to block him out of my mind.

"Fionna, how old are you?" I asked her, changing the subject.

"I'm twenty-one. Why?"

"What do you do besides work here?"

"I take classes at TCC in the evening."

"Good. Stay in school and keep working, honey, because men will come and go. And tomorrow is never promised. As long as you live by those two rules, you will be all right."

"You know what's so funny?"

"No. What is it?"

"I grew up wanting to be just like Sunshine because she had everything a woman could ever want. Her car was nice, and her apartment was laced with the most expensive leather furniture. She even had all the top designers' clothing in her closet. When Chanel came out with a new handbag and the shoes to match, Sunshine made sure she got it before anyone else got it. And what made her stick out in a crowd was, she had a body to die for. She could've had any man she wanted, and she knew it.

"But when the police came to my mama's house that night and told us they found her naked body shot up underneath the sheets of a bed that belonged to some guy named Quincy, I was devastated. And from that very day, I looked at her differently. She was no longer my idol. She reminded me of a prostitute, and that wasn't how I wanted to live my life. It was bad enough that she caught that fed charge for stashing all Ricky's drugs inside her new salon, but then to come home from jail and get caught up in some more mess behind a guy my family had never met blew our minds. We weren't ready for that."

"I'm sure y'all weren't. But you've got to remember that our lives are already planned. And all we're supposed to do is walk down the path marked for us."

"Yeah, I heard my mama saying something like that before, but I still think we can stop things from happening."

"I believe that too."

She smiled at me. "I don't know why Sunshine said she didn't like you, because you seem cool to me."

Just then a bell went off inside the merchant machine. She and I both looked down and realized the machine was finally working, so she processed my transaction and gave me a copy of the receipt. I moved to the side and allowed her to take care of the other customers.

When my order came up, she signaled for me to come back up to the counter area. She handed me a small white bag with my sandwich inside, and then she handed me my sweet iced tea. Before I turned to leave, she leaned over the counter and said, "Take care of yourself."

I gave her a half-smile. "And you do the same," I told her, and then I left.

When I got back across the street, I headed back to Tony's car. He was sitting in the driver's seat. I got inside the car and let out a loud sigh.

He looked at me. "Are you all right?"

"Yes, I'm fine."

Tony turned the key to start the car and drove out of the lot.

I turned my head to look out the passenger side window and instantly thought back on everything Fionna had said about Sunshine. It was funny how life threw curve balls at you when you least expected it. Fionna had admired Sunshine all her life, but the day Sunshine no longer reigned supreme and was caught with her pants down, Fionna saw her for what she truly was.

Tony merged back on the road and headed down Tidewater Drive toward Princess Anne Road. The whole drive to his next destination was done in complete silence. The traffic was somewhat congested, but Tony maneuvered his way through it, and before I even realized it, we were sitting at a red light at the corner of Tidewater Drive and St. Julian, right near the Huntersville subdivision.

While Tony proceeded to his destination, all sorts of thoughts ran through my mind. I was starting to get anxious, and was ready to get out of Virginia. Listening to the CD by The Game that he was playing only made me even more uptight. Every lyric talked about murdering somebody, chopping up their bodies, and sending their remains to their families. And Tony was bopping his head to the beat.

I tried desperately to block it out and slip into another zone, but it didn't work. Thankfully, his cell started ringing, so he had to turn down the volume to hear the caller.

"I'm right around the corner," he said. "I'll be there in a minute . . . Ai'ght, I can do that."

After ending the call, Tony pressed down on the accelerator. I didn't know where he was going, but wherever it was, I knew he was trying to beat the time he had given that person. I sat there quietly thinking about how badly I couldn't wait to get back to the hotel, but to make that happen, I had to get back to Tony's apartment to pick up my rental.

After several turns Tony finally pulled over to the side of B Avenue in front of this old, run-down house. It was the fifth house from the corner, and it stood out among the rest of homes. As I looked at the house, it reminded me of a stash house Ricky used to have. Old houses like this never attracted the police because they looked abandoned. The only way a cop would run up in a spot like this particular one was if someone ratted it out. Other than that, anyone who managed to set up shop would make tons of dough without any interruptions.

I watched Tony park his car and turn off the ignition. He looked over at me and said, "Come on. Let's go."

Caught off guard, I looked back at him. "Where are we going?"

"Inside my homeboy's house."

I turned my head to look at the house, and then I turned back around to look at Tony. "You have got to be kidding!" I said. "I am not stepping foot inside that house. It looks just like a crackhouse."

"Kira, it ain't no crackhouse."

"Well, if it isn't a crackhouse, then it's got to be a stash house, because I can't see somebody living there." I took another look at the house, and then I looked back at Tony.

"Look, I don't know what else to tell you, but I do know that I'm gon' be in there for a spell, so if you want to sit in the car and take the chance of getting struck by one of these niggas' stray bullets, then that's on you." He then got out of the car and slammed the driver's door.

I thought about what he said for a brief second and realized that he might be right for a change. I was in the heart of Huntersville where niggas would put a pistol up to their own brother's head if they had to, so how would I be able to escape that? The fear of losing my life came crashing down on me really heavy. Not to mention, I couldn't risk someone else recognizing me. That would definitely be suicidal. So, without saying another word, I opened the passenger side door, hopped out of the car, and closed the door behind me.

After we climbed all nine steps that connected to the front porch, Tony rushed toward the front door.

A tall, slim, brown-skinned chick opened the door

and stood in the doorway waiting for Tony and me to enter the house. Once we were inside, she closed the door behind us.

I stood there beside Tony and waited to see what he would do next.

She looked at him and greeted him. "What's up?"

I thought she would've acknowledged me by saying hello or giving me a nod, but she didn't look my way. I purposely cleared my throat and said hello, but she acted as if I didn't exist.

After she locked the front door she told Tony to follow her. Like the caboose on a train, I trotted behind them. The hallway wasn't too long, but it looked really creepy. We walked on old hardwood floors that felt worn-out and very loose. I thought a couple of the boards were going to give out on us, so I tried to tread lightly.

Finally we entered a back room, where two big black guys sat at a round table counting a massive amount of money. They had to be high school football players in their earlier years, because both of those guys reminded me of the late, great Bernie Mac, except one had a bald head, and the other one had long dreadlocks. From what I could see, they both wore dark-colored jeans, black hoodies, and black Nike boots.

"Today looks like payday to me." Tony commented.

Both men smiled at Tony but didn't say a word. I thought it was really weird that no one wanted to talk. I felt uncomfortable as I stood beside Tony. I wanted him to take care of what he had to do, so we could leave.

"Kira, you can have a seat if you want to," he told me.

I took a quick glimpse at the raggedy, old sofa he told me to sit on and told him that I was fine standing up.

"You sure? Because I'm gon' be here at least twenty minutes."

"Yeah, I'm sure," I assured him, my feet glued to where I was standing.

The chick who had opened the front door left the room. I heard her walk back down the hallway and then head upstairs. Then Tony walked over to the table and stood beside one of the guys.

I watched and waited for Tony to hand them something, but he didn't. Instead he held out his hand, and the baldheaded guy handed him a large sum of cash. From what I could see, Tony must've been given at least five grand. Every bill he had in his hand was either a fifty- or hundred-dollar bill. I couldn't see Tony's expression because his back was to me, but I knew he must have been extremely happy. During all the years I had known him, I knew he had never held that much money in his hands at one time. I was sure he felt like he'd won the lottery.

As he stood at the table counting his money, I heard footsteps coming down the stairs. I knew it was the chick coming back downstairs, so I didn't bother to turn around. I wanted to keep my eyes on Tony and these two overgrown rejects posted up before me.

The footsteps grew louder, so I knew it would be only a matter of seconds before she graced the room once again with her presence. I heard her steps draw closer as she put one foot in front of the other, but then all of a sudden she stopped.

I felt her presence behind me, but I didn't know how close she was. My curiosity went into overdrive as I wondered why she'd come to an abrupt stop. I forced myself not to turn around, because I didn't want to seem like I was being nosy. But I couldn't help myself. I had to find out what she was doing.

Just as I got up the nerve to turn around, I got a glimpse of a black piece of fabric. I knew it wasn't something attached to the wall because I would have seen it when I first came into the house. So what was it? I turned my head to the right to see what this black thing looming over me was.

Without any warning, everything around me turned pitch-black. I realized my head had just been covered with a dark, cotton bag. I panicked and tried to pull the bag off my head. "What the fuck is going on?" I screamed. "Take this shit off me! Tony, help me!"

No one responded. The next thing I knew, I was struck in the back of my head with some heavy object and knocked out cold.

PLAYING
MIND GAMES

I was tired of being hit in my fucking head. It hadn't been two months since my cousin Nikki and Fatu' had knocked me out and had me tied up in a fucking warehouse. And now here I was again being held against my will. I couldn't see a damn thing, but I knew there were at least three people in the room with me. My head was still covered with the same black bag, and my mouth was covered with some kind of tape. They must have taped my mouth while I was unconscious so that, when I regained consciousness, I wouldn't blow up their spot by yelling and screaming.

I tried to move a little bit, because I wanted whoever was in the room to know I was indeed conscious. I actually had to use the bathroom, and I wanted to see if they would remove the cover from my head. I turned my head from left to right so I could get their attention.

I didn't know who was talking, but one of the guys said, "She's up." His voice was a very deep baritone.

I noticed he had a Southern accent. He sounded like he was born and raised in Virginia. I played his voice over and over in my mind to see if I recognized it, but I kept coming up empty-handed. I tried moving my feet, but they were taped too.

"Whatcha think we should do with her?" he asked.

"Just leave her ass where she's at! It ain't like she can get up and go somewhere," another male voice replied.

"Yeah, nigga, I guess your dumb ass is right!" the first guy said, laughing.

The humor made me sick to my stomach, but I guess they were in a position to laugh since their life wasn't hanging in the balance. I would have given away my life savings to be in their shoes right then. Having three against one made me realize that the odds were against me. I couldn't believe I was right back where I'd started. I could never seem to get my life right. I could kick myself for coming back to Virginia. I knew it was a bad idea to fly there, but, nah, I listened to my uncle and came anyway.

I guess all the times I'd cheated death, had caught up with me. Sitting there waiting for the inevitable was something really scary. I had no idea who was going to take my life, but I knew it would be sometime soon.

The urge to use the bathroom got more and more intense. I started to say fuck it and urinate on myself, but the thought of humiliating myself before I took my last breath made me decide against it. I continued to move my head back and forth to see if I could get someone's attention, and this time it finally worked.

The sack was pulled off my head and I was greeted by the big, husky, baldhead guy. The light in the room suddenly blinded me. I closed my eyes tightly to allow my eyes time to get readjusted. When I opened my eyes again, I looked this guy straight in his eyes. I tried desperately to talk while I had my mouth taped up, but all it sounded like was loud mumbling. A few seconds later, he snatched off the tape.

"Ouch!" I screamed. The pain was agonizing. And the fucked-up thing about it was, I couldn't use my hands to massage my mouth because they were tied behind my back. At that moment I remembered that I had a utility knife in the side pocket of my purse. If only I could find my purse, I would be able to free myself.

"Whatcha want?" he asked me.

I could tell he was a little irritated, but before I answered him, I scanned the entire room to see who was there. There were two guys, and the chick from earlier was nowhere in sight.

"I need to use the bathroom really badly," I said, hoping the men would be sympathetic to my bathroom needs.

"I'm sorry, but I can't let you get up," he said, not sounding sorry at all.

"So what am I supposed to do, just sit here and piss on myself?"

"You can if you want," he replied.

Since I wasn't getting anywhere with this asshole, I looked across the room to the other guy to see if he would cut me some slack. "Hey, look, I've got to use the bathroom really badly, so can you please tell this guy to untie me so I can go?" I asked, displaying the saddest expression I could muster.

"Sorry, but I can't override his decision," the other guy said. Obviously, he couldn't care less about my problem.

The guy standing over me with the tape in his hand leaned toward me to put it back on.

I stopped him in his tracks. "Hey, can I ask you a quick question?"

"What is it?"

"Look, it's obvious that I'm not going to get out of here alive, so can you just please have a heart and let me use the bathroom? It's not like I'm gonna try to escape or anything."

"That's not what I'm worried about."

"Then what are you worried about? Because all I have to do is pee, and that won't take nothing but two minutes."

The guy looked down at me for a complete five seconds. Then he looked over at the other guy. I turned to look at the other guy too. His facial expression stayed the same.

"It's up to you, dog," the guy sitting on the couch finally said.

The guy in front of me turned his attention back to me. "A'ight, I'ma let you go, but don't try no funny shit, or I'm gon' kill you my damn self!" he warned me.

"Thank you so much," I said.

I sat there patiently while he untied the rope from my wrists and ankles. I don't know how long I'd been unconscious, but from the numbness in my legs, I could tell that it had been at least an hour, if not longer.

When I stood, my legs felt like they were going to give way. "I don't think I'm gonna be able to walk on my own," I told the guy.

"I can carry you if you want," he said.

"How would you do that?"

"I can throw you over my shoulders."

The thought of him lifting me up and carrying me over his shoulders wasn't what I really wanted, so I decided to tough it out and walk on my own. Honestly, I didn't want him touching me. I wasn't about to let him get a cheap feel off me. I figured if it was time for my life to be over, I should go out with some dignity.

"Never mind. I can manage," I assured him.

I took the first step with my right foot, and then I took the next step with my left, treading very lightly until the numbness went away altogether. With each step I took, the more the feeling in my legs came back. I knew one thing. If I even had the desire to make an attempt to escape, my plans would be over before I blinked my eyes.

"Which way is the bathroom?" I asked as we reached the entrance of the hallway.

"It's that door right there on the right." He pointed in the direction of the kitchen. When I noticed the bathroom was less than twelve feet from the room where these assholes had me tied up, I knew there was no possible way to escape.

As I approached the bathroom door, he reached for the doorknob and opened the door for me. Then he switched on the light.

I stood at the entrance, peered inside, and got an eyeful. I looked at the guy and asked him if this was the only bathroom in the house.

He looked back at me and laughed. "There's one upstairs. But what's wrong with this one?"

"What's wrong with it?" I asked in a sarcastic tone.

He knew how fucked-up this bathroom was. The smell of the urine was so strong, it damn near killed me at the door. The toilet seat looked brown and rusted, and the sink had the same discoloration. I even saw a couple roaches scatter, like they were trying to run for cover. There was no toilet paper in sight, but there was half a roll of paper towels. I guess I was supposed to use that to wipe my ass. The few pieces of tile on the floor looked like they were about to come up. It was so bad that the wooden floor underneath was visible. Too bad there wasn't a window, because this shit needed airing out big time.

"Hey, look, I ain't going way upstairs so you can use the bathroom. If you don't use this one, then you ain't using nothing."

I sucked my teeth because I saw that I wasn't getting anywhere with this conversation. His big lazy ass didn't want to walk up upstairs, so I had to suffer with the wretched and sordid conditions of this bathroom.

I knew I had to hold my breath while I was inside that dungeon, but I also knew I couldn't hold my breath longer than a good thirty seconds, so I rushed into the bathroom and closed the door. I don't know how I did it, but I pulled up my dress, squatted, and pissed all over the nasty seat. I didn't do it purposely. It just happened that way. I was mad that I'd pissed all over the seat and the floor, because that meant I had to be the one to wipe it up, and I didn't want to touch anything in there. It didn't matter that I could use the paper towels. The idea of being in this hellhole longer than I had to be definitely gave me the creeps.

I grabbed the roll of paper towels, snatched off a sheet with which to wipe myself, and then placed the roll back on the edge of the sink. After I wiped myself, I used the same sheet to wipe off the toilet seat. I knew that was nasty and not hygienic, but look where I was. This whole fucking place was a dump. So why should I treat it any better than they did?

Almost about to run out of breath, I dropped the used paper towel into the toilet and flushed. Not even a second later, I burst through the bathroom door and was back in the hallway standing beside the same asshole who wouldn't let me use the upstairs bathroom. He didn't waste any time escorting my ass back to the room where they had me tied up.

When we reentered the room, I noticed that the stupid-ass chick had found her way there and was sitting on the sofa closest to the chair where I was tied, and sifting through the contents of my two-thousand-dollar Chanel handbag. I couldn't believe how casually she handled my wallet as she flipped through my credit cards and my driver's license.

"She won't be needing this or this after tonight," she said.

I started to curse her ass out and tell her to leave my shit alone, but instead I looked at her like she was beneath me, and then I rolled my eyes.

"What the fuck was all that?" she blurted out.

I ignored her ass, like she wasn't talking to me.

That made her mad, because she repeated herself, and this time she said it with much attitude. "I know you heard me talking to you when I asked you what the fuck was all that!"

"Who you talking to?" the guy standing beside me asked her.

"I'm talking to that bitch!" she screamed.

I sat back down on the chair, and while the guy was tying my arms behind me, he started laughing at the chick. I knew I wasn't in any position to start some shit with her, so I tried my best to ignore her comments, but of course, she wasn't having that.

"I'm not gonna ask you again," she roared. She stood and walked over to where I was sitting.

I looked up at her. "What do you want me to say?"

"Don't play fucking games with me! Just tell me why the fuck you gritted on me like you got beef with me or something."

"I didn't grit on you," I lied.

"Oh, so now I'm seeing things, huh?"

"Kasey, go ahead on with that bullshit!" the other guy yelled out. "You see she ain't trying to go there with you."

"Fuck that! She already went there!" she yelled.

"Girl, sit your ass down," the guy tying me up said.

She sucked her teeth, grabbed a fistful of my hair, and tugged.

"Oowww! What the fuck is your problem?" I screamed and gave her the nastiest expression I could muster. If I wasn't tied up, and this nigga wasn't standing between us, I would have smacked the hell out of her. With all the fucking mouth she had, she was really overdue for a good, old-fashioned beatdown, and I would have been the perfect candidate to give it to her.

"You look at me again like you just did, then I'ma show you my problem." Then she walked back over to the sofa and sat down.

I was furious with that bitch! I really couldn't say what the hell I wanted to, because I would've given her an earful. The fact that she grabbed and yanked on my hair really blew my fucking mind. She had balls the size of a man to do something like that. And the fact that I couldn't do anything about it also blew my mind. But what else could I do?

When this overgrown-ass nigga finished tying me back up, he grabbed the roll of gray electric tape to cover my mouth. I didn't want that shit over my mouth again, so I said, "Please, I promise, I won't say a word."

"Don't listen to that shit, Dré. Tape her ass up!" Kasey said.

Dré looked over at the other guy. "What's up? Put the tape back on or what?"

The other guy was rolling marijuana into some blunt paper, and it seemed like he didn't want to be bothered with any of the decision-making. He looked at Dré. "Nigga, I don't care what you do."

Getting the green light to do whatever he wanted, Dré decided not to tape my mouth again.

Kasey made it known she was pissed. "Try to yell one time, bitch, and I'ma personally fuck you up!"

After she made that comment, I didn't bother to look her way. I was more focused on how I was going to get out of this hellhole. I wanted to live another day, so my mind was on figuring out a way to escape the jaws of death. I had no idea why they were holding me captive, or who they were holding me for. I needed answers, and the way my captors were acting, I didn't think I was gonna get them anytime soon.

Now, I knew that sorry-ass Tony set me up, and that the money Dré gave him was the payoff for delivering me. So wherever that bastard was, I hoped the next time he stepped foot outside his car, he got run over. What he did to me was really foul. No matter how I felt about someone, I wouldn't serve them up to get killed, unless they did something to put me in harm's way. Like my dead husband Ricky and his partner Russ.

Ricky wanted me dead because I wouldn't help him set up Papi. And Russ's crooked ass robbed me of all my life's savings, purchased a fucking Bentley, and then when I ran into him and confronted him, he pulled out a pistol on me. Now how fucked-up was that?

But my problem was, I was too damn forgiving and trusting. I let people fuck me over at least twenty times before I left them alone completely. And that was just plain crazy. Who did that? I couldn't say where I got that mentality, but that wasn't how I should be. I mean, look at the situation I was in now. I was too fucking trusting of Tony. I allowed that lowlife-ass nigga to serve me up to these other lowlives. Who knew what plans they had for me? Whatever they were, I knew it wouldn't be pretty.

Someone knocked on the front door, and my heart damn near leaped out of my fucking chest. I figured maybe whoever it was had come there for me.

Kasey hopped up from the sofa and raced to the front door. Before the person could knock a second time, she opened the door.

As soon as the person entered the house, I heard footsteps walking in my direction. The closer the sounds of the footsteps, the more uneasy I felt. If my hands weren't tied up, I probably would have chewed off all of my fingernails.

A few seconds later, Kasey walked back into the room, with the visitor two steps behind her. It became obvious that everyone was expecting this person to come here, because neither one of the guys asked Kasey who had arrived. I was the only person left in the fucking dark, so I had to wait and see.

When I saw that the visitor was Uncle Lanier, I was a little confused. At first I wanted to jump for joy, but then when I looked at the menacing expression on his face, I realized he wasn't there to set me free.

He walked slowly toward me, a cynical smile on his

face. He looked like a fucking mechanic, dressed in a pair of blue overalls, but I knew he would never get his hands dirty to work on anyone's car. He was never the type to get his hands dirty and always paid people to do his dirty work for him.

"I know you must have a ton of thoughts running through your head, huh?" he asked me.

I didn't respond because I wanted to see where he was going with this.

"Oh, so now you have nothing to say?" He took a couple more steps toward me.

I honestly wanted to respond, but what I wanted to say would've probably come out wrong, so I sat still and remained quiet.

"Aren't you wondering why I'm here?"

This time I tried to say something, but my mouth wouldn't budge. My eyes got extremely watery, and before I knew it, one tear after the next fell down my face.

"Ahhh, don't cry," he said, and then he stroked my hair with his fingers.

I literally caught chills and wanted to vomit. "Don't touch me!" I snapped.

Without any forewarning, Kasey smacked the shit out of me. I couldn't see it, but I knew my face turned beet-red.

"Didn't I tell you I was going to fuck you up if you said one word out cha mouth?" she roared.

I got to be frank. I was furious as hell when that bitch put her fucking hands on me. I wanted to get up and teach that whore a lesson. "I don't give a fuck what you said! But I do know you better not put your filthy hands on me again."

Kasey stepped toward me and raised her hand again to whack me once more, but my uncle grabbed her hand right before she struck me. "Kasey, I got this. Go have a seat."

She snatched her hand from my uncle's grip, rolling her eyes and sucking her teeth as she stormed away. "Lucky bitch!" she said, gritting her teeth.

Both Dré and the other guy sat back with grins on their faces. They must've thought that little fit Kasey was throwing was humorous. I didn't think the shit was funny at all. Everybody in here needed their fucking heads blown off, because none of them was dealing with full decks.

My uncle really shocked me, though. I sat there and racked my brain trying to figure out why the fuck he was in on this bullshit. I mean, come on! I had always been taught that blood was thicker than water. So why the fuck had he set me up? We were family. I was his fucking niece, for God's sake! Where was the fucking love? I now realized that he had planned this shit with Tony way before I came to town. Which explained why he'd pressed the issue for me to come to the funeral. Now that was some grimy shit!

For the life of me, I couldn't come up with a logical explanation for why my uncle would do this to me. He was always like a fucking father to me. I couldn't count how many times he'd had my back in situations I couldn't get out of. We did drift apart when I got married to Ricky, but we still kept in touch. I knew he hated the type of man Ricky was, and since I wasn't about to let go of my husband at the time, he pretty much took the leash off me and wished me luck.

I guess the straw that broke the camel's back was when Nikki got arrested. He didn't say anything to me at the time, but I knew he was angry. Nikki's mother basically talked for the both of them. She hated the whole idea of Nikki being around me, especially when she found out that Nikki got hooked up with that Syncere, who turned out to be a psycho, and then he tried to kill Nikki. So my uncle's wife never let me live down that one. I don't know how many times I tried to convince both of her parents that I had no hand in introducing those two. Nikki had met him on her own, but they refused to believe that, so I just threw up my hands and said fuck it.

Then Nikki left town with me so we could start a new life together, and she ended up being murdered. How fucked-up could that be? I knew it looked like every time Nikki was around me, bad things happened to her, but really all those bad things were Nikki's own fault. Now it looked like I would pay with my life for all of Nikki's stupid mistakes.

"I want everyone to leave this room," my uncle instructed.

And like flunkies, everyone got up from where they were sitting and walked out of the room. When the room was completely empty, he grabbed one of the metal chairs that was placed at the table a few feet away and placed it directly in front of me. He took a seat and faced me.

Looking me straight in the eyes, he said, "You know Nikki was all I had after your grandmother was murdered, right?"

Once again I ignored him.

"You know what, I tried to convince myself that you had nothing to do with my baby getting murdered, but then I thought about everything you said to me and the police, and it just didn't add up. Now that I've got you all to myself, I know you're gonna tell me what really happened to my daughter."

I sat there and watched my uncle while he talked to me, and he displayed no emotions whatsoever. If my eyes were closed, I wouldn't have known who the fuck he was. He looked and sounded very sinister. I couldn't believe he had these people holding me hostage so he could find out what had really happened to Nikki. Unfortunately, there was no way I could come clean with him. Telling him I was with Nikki when she got killed would implicate me. He could then use that information against me and have my ass put behind bars for being an accessory to murder. My life would be completely fucked up. Everything I'd built for myself back in Anguilla would be a waste. My fiancé, the house I bought, my new car, it would all go up in smoke.

"So what will it be?" he asked, his expression remaining unchanged.

"Uncle Lanier," I began, my voice barely audible, "I don't know what happened to Nikki. She and I lost touch with each other before I left the country."

Suddenly he wrapped his right hand around my neck

and nearly choked me to death. "That's a lie!" he roared. The veins in his temple looked like they were about to pop. I'd never seen my uncle like this before.

Gasping for air and trying to talk at the same time, I begged him to let me go. I knew he couldn't understand what I was saying, but he saw the tears fall from my eyes, so he had to know I was in pain.

He finally released me, but I needed more relief. I wanted to massage my neck with my hands, but they were still tied behind my back, so I was left with no other choice but to sit there in excruciating pain as he plotted his next move.

"Kira, I'm only gonna say this one more time," he said calmly. "If you don't come clean with me about what happened to Nikki, you are really going to be sorry."

I thought for a second more after he gave me the ultimatum. I wondered what he would do to me if I continued to act like I knew nothing about Nikki's murder. It was unclear to me what he was capable of doing, but when I thought about how intense the pressure was when he wrapped his hand around my throat, I knew he was capable of hurting me. The other thought that popped into my mind was whether he had any intentions of killing me. He hadn't made that clear to me at all, so that was something I needed to know.

"Uncle Lanier, what do you plan on doing to me?" I asked, tears still falling down my face.

"If you don't tell me what happened to my daughter, I'm gonna kill you," he replied without blinking an eye.

I heard the sincerity in his voice and knew he was as serious as cancer. But I couldn't stop wondering how he got this way. I'd known this man my entire fucking life. He used to remind me about how he changed my fucking diapers when I was a baby, and now he was sitting in front of me threatening to take my life.

One part of me believed he was serious, but the other part of me thought he was bluffing. He was my uncle, my mother's only brother; we had the same blood pumping through our veins, so I couldn't imagine him killing me.

Confused about whether I still had a leg to stand on, I decided to call his bluff. Telling him that I'd witnessed Nikki's murder, even though I didn't pull the trigger, would be devastating to me. Not only that, but I knew he wouldn't understand if I told him that she had turned against me and fucked my fiancé. She was his baby—the only seed he had. So in his eyes she couldn't do anything wrong.

Whatever I decided to say, I knew it had to sound convincing. I took a deep breath and exhaled. Tears fell more rapidly from my eyes. "Uncle Lanier, I swear on my life, I don't know who killed—"

Once again he drove his fingers into my neck, even more savagely than before. He literally sank his fingers deeper and deeper into my flesh.

I began to cough hoarsely as the breath was violently squeezed from my body. Fear overpowered me. I wanted nothing more than for him to let me go so I could coax air back into my heaving chest. I knew it would be just another second before I expired because I started blacking out.

When he realized that I was passing out, his chokehold relaxed, and he released his hand from my neck. My throat was racked with pain, and I knew it must look really raw and discolored. Able to breathe again, I gasped for more oxygen as he stood there and watched.

"You think I'm fucking playing with you? I will fucking kill you, bitch! Stop playing with me and tell me who killed my fucking daughter!"

Through my watery eyes, I could still see him hovering over me. As I began to breathe a little more easily, he lunged back and slammed his fist into the side of my right cheek, drawing blood. "Tell me now!" he yelled.

"OK. OK."

Finally getting his attention, he took a step back and crossed his arms. "I'm listening," he said.

I tried to collect my thoughts, but everything was all scrambled up in my mind. Words were jumbled over each other, and I couldn't think straight. I looked down to the floor, and then I looked back at him. Something told me that he knew I knew what really happened to Nikki, and that was why he wasn't letting up. It was like he could see right through me. I needed to say something he wanted to hear.

I looked down at the floor once again and said a silent prayer asking God for a miracle. I asked Him to deliver me from this situation, and I told Him I didn't care how

He did it, just as long as it was done. I cried out to Him through my aching heart, and was hoping He heard me.

I looked back up, and my uncle still stood there, waiting. I quickly reminded myself that I had to look at this situation from another angle. I wasn't dealing with a rational man. He wasn't the man I grew up with and called Uncle Lanier. This guy was cut from a different cloth, and he was out for my blood.

Right before I attempted to open my mouth, Kasey ran back into the room. She said, "Hey, L.L., Dré said hold tight for a minute because the police are in front of the house fucking with them young boys who sell them red bags."

My uncle turned around and gave her his full attention. From my point of view, she couldn't have come at a better time. I looked to the ceiling and thanked God. People said He looked out for babies and fools, and they were right.

"How long have they been out there fucking with them?" he asked.

"They just pulled up about three minutes ago."

"Stay right here and watch her," he instructed, and then he rushed off.

I heard him as he hurried down the hallway and up the staircase. I let out of sigh of relief as his footsteps grew fainter.

Knowing that the police were standing outside gave me the urge to yell out for help, but then I figured, if I opened my mouth, my uncle would punish me for it.

Not only that, I was unsure of how close they were to the house. It would be just my luck that they wouldn't hear me. I knew if I was ever going to get out of this, it wouldn't be because the police saved me. That was shit you only saw on TV.

After Uncle Lanier left, Kasey had a smirk plastered on her face like she'd seen something amusing. I wanted so badly to ask her what the fuck was funny, but I didn't have any strength left in me to open my mouth. I could feel blood running from my lips and my mouth like a faucet. All I could do was sit there and pray to walk out of this place alive.

"Damn, homegirl! He really fucked you up!" she commented as she stood before me, her hands pressed against her hips.

I looked at her, and then I turned my head away. She wasn't worth any of the time I had left. My focus had to be on trying to figure out a good-ass lie to tell my uncle. The shit couldn't be farfetched, so I went into thinking mode. But once again, this dumb bitch interrupted me. I started to tell her to get lost, but that would have been grounds for her to put her hands on me, and I wasn't in the mood for that bullshit. I wanted to keep every ounce of energy I had left to use when my uncle got back.

"Bitch, don't act like you can't hear me!" she yelled.

"Kasey, why do you keep taunting me? You see how helpless I am right now. I don't have the energy to start a confrontation with you. If you beat me until I was black and blue, I would just sit here and pray to God that you'd have mercy on me."

"Don't try to make me feel sorry for you. I heard what kind of chick you were, Ms. Thang. Yeah, L.L. gave us the rundown on you and your husband Ricky, and how y'all turned y'all backs on Nikki after she got locked up for transporting y'all shit." She frowned. "That was some foul shit, if you ask me! Niggas like that get dealt with when they do that betraying shit!"

Listening to Kasey talk me to death with all that misinformation gave me a headache to go with the pain I felt in my throat. She made matters worse when she said that I deserved to be in this situation because a lot of other people suffered at the hands of me and Ricky. She even went as far as to say that she heard how vicious Ricky was when he used to run the streets, but when it came to women, he was soft.

"I remember when my homegirl told me that he tried to get her," she said. "She used to bartend at Blakely's. Every time he walked up in there with his boys, she told me that he always tried to get her to call him, but she said she wouldn't take his number."

"I'm not surprised," I replied nonchalantly. At this point Ricky was dead, so his past life didn't affect me at all. I couldn't care less about anything he used to do. All that shit I went through with him was behind me.

"Oh, so you knew your husband wasn't shit, huh?"

I didn't respond. To me it was somewhat rhetorical, especially if what she said was true. I really didn't want to entertain her anymore, so I closed my eyes and laid my head against the back of the chair.

Finally I heard my uncle's footsteps coming back toward us. An uneasy feeling crept back into my stomach, and my heart started racing. He was coming back to finish what he'd started, and I knew he was going to punish me.

My eyes grew every bit of two more inches when I saw him enter the room. His facial expression hadn't changed one bit. He looked like he had come back to take care of business, so I knew I was about to embark on another rocky experience.

"Kasey, I want you to come ride with me and Dré uptown," he said.

"Is the police still outside?" she asked him.

"No. They just left."

"Whatcha gon' do with her?" she asked him.

"Breon is gonna watch her."

"A'ight," she said and left the room.

As soon as Kasey walked out of the room, my uncle walked over to me. I was literally shaking on the inside and prepared for whatever he was about to say or do. I looked directly in his eyes. I wanted to burst into tears and beg him to release me, but I knew that wasn't about to happen, so I left well enough alone. I did, however, get up the nerve to ask him what he planned to do with me.

He looked at me and said, "Get the truth."

"Are you going to let me go?"

"Yeah. As soon as you tell me the truth."

"But I've been telling you truth."

He leaned over into my face and said in a low whisper, "You and I both know you're holding something back, so the sooner you come clean with it, the sooner you can leave here."

He stood straight up, but before he turned to leave the room, he encouraged me to think about what he'd said because when he got back my time would be up.

When the other guy, Breon, walked into the room, my uncle walked out and headed toward the front door. I heard him say a few words to Kasey and Dré when he got to the front door.

As soon as I heard the front door open and close, I knew they had left. What they were about to go get into was a complete mystery to me.

WHEN ALL ELSE FAILS

Breon sat down on the sofa about seven feet away from me. He picked up the remote control and surfed through the channels. He stopped at channel 28, A&E. *The First 48* was on, and his eyes were glued to the screen. I'd watched the show a few times before moving out of the country. I guess now wasn't such a bad time to do some catching up, since I was being held there against my will.

As I sat there, my stomach started growling. I never ate my sandwich from Feather-N-Fin. If I knew Tony had intentions to leave me, I would have eaten it before I got out of the car. I didn't know how long I'd been there, but through the thin curtains that covered the windows I noticed that the street lights were on outside, so I knew it was past my dinner time.

Breon was so engrossed in his show, I was afraid to ask him for something to eat. But my stomach persisted with the rumbling.

"Excuse me," I said to get his attention.

He turned and looked at me. "Yeah, what's up?"

"I know you probably think I'm crazy for asking you this, but I was hoping you could get me something to snack on, because I am starving over here."

He hesitated for a moment. "I was told not to leave this room for nothing," he said. "But I guess I can get you something."

Knowing that this guy wasn't all that bad made me happy for the moment. I gave him a half-smile. "Thanks."

He walked out of the room and returned a minute later with a piece of chicken wrapped in a paper towel and a clear plastic cup of red juice. "I got you a piece of some KFC we had earlier, so it's room temperature, and I got you some fruit punch to go with it."

"Thank you so much!" I replied. I was happy as hell when he walked in the room with that shit in his hands. I knew he wouldn't untie me so I could feed myself, so I didn't ask. At this point, all that mattered was that I was about to put something on my stomach. Well, maybe that wasn't all that mattered because, if he untied me and told me I could leave, I'd leave that cold piece of chicken behind in a flash. But that wasn't happening.

Breon approached me with the chicken in his right hand and the cup of fruit punch in the other. He held the piece of chicken right in front of my mouth so I could bite it. I chewed, and then I bit into it again.

Under normal circumstances I would have felt really stupid letting some complete stranger feed me a cold piece of chicken, but unfortunately the situation I was in wasn't normal, so I refused to complain.

Once I had devoured the entire piece of chicken, he pressed the cup of juice between my lips. I opened my mouth just enough to drink. It didn't take me long to drink the entire cup of fruit punch, and when I was done I let out a loud belch. "Excuse me," I said.

Breon smiled. "You ain't got to apologize. You a'ight," he assured me as he held the chicken bone in one hand, and the empty plastic cup in the other. Without asking me, he used the napkin he'd held the chicken with and wiped the grease and the red ring of juice off my mouth. I was speechless. But when I got back my voice I thanked him once again.

He smiled again. "I told you, you a'ight."

"I know. But I can't help it. The way I've been treated since I've been here is far worse than I've ever been treated in my life, especially by a family member." I waited for Breon to make a comment, but he just shrugged his shoulders and gave me a blank expression.

It really didn't surprise me that he didn't want to respond. The entire time I'd been here he was the only one who acted like he didn't want to be part of the decisions when it came to me. And now that I looked at him closer, he seemed like he was a little standoffish. People like him preferred not to get into situations that didn't concern them. I was like that too, so I guess he and I had something in common.

I watched him as he strolled back into the kitchen area to dispose of the paper towel and the empty plastic cup. When he came back into the room, he sat back down on the sofa and resumed watching *The First 48*. I tuned back in, but I couldn't help but think how long it would be before my uncle, Kasey, and Dré came back. The thought of them coming back to torture me some more made me uneasy. The food and drink I had just consumed was bound to come back up if I thought about it any longer. Talking to Breon would definitely take my mind off him.

"Hey, Breon," I said.

He took his eyes off the television and gave me his undivided attention. "What's up?"

"How do you know my uncle?"

"Me and my brother Dré met him through our cousin Tony right after his baby mama Rhonda got killed. I'm not sure how they met, but I heard it was during the time when the homicide detectives went to Nikki and started asking her questions about the murder, since Rhonda was snatched up from the hair shop. But, besides that, me and Dré copped a couple of brand-new flat-screen TVs from him a while back. He told us he was the district manager for Wal-Mart, so he could get us anything we wanted for the right price. When he called us last week and told us he had some brand-new laptops he needed to get rid of, we called our homeboy Mitch and he took 'em off L.L.'s hands with no problem."

I got quiet for a second. I had to mull over what Breon had just said. Uncle Lanier was always a straight-laced guy. I'd never seen him associate with any thugs, so what did he and Tony have in common? I decided to put that question on the back burner for now and get as much information out of Breon as possible.

"Do you know where they just went?"

"Yeah. L.L. got a call from some nigga from the Wal-Mart warehouse, so he had to go."

"Why did he need your brother and Kasey to go with him?

"Well, he needed Kasey to drive, and he needed my brother to help him load some shit onto his truck."

Getting information from Breon was easier than stealing candy from a baby. Every question I asked, he answered. I had just a couple more questions for him, so I held no punches.

"Kasey must be y'all sister, because she looks just like y'all," I commented, hoping he'd confirm or deny my suspicions.

"Nah, she ain't our sister. She's our cousin."

"How old is she?"

"She either just turned twenty-seven, or she's gon' be twenty-seven soon, because Dré is three years older than her."

"Does she have any kids?"

"Nah. She ain't got no kids."

"What about you?"

"Yeah, I got two children."

"Boys or girls?"

"I got a little man and I got a little girl."

"Does your son look like you?"

"He sure does."

"What about your daughter? I bet she's really pretty."

Breon smiled. The thought of his little girl made his

eyes sparkle. "Yeah, she's a cutie, but she's bad as hell. You know how terrible twos can be."

"I don't have any kids, but I've seen enough two-year-olds to know what you're talking about," I said. "So what's their names?"

I continued to make small talk with this guy because I wanted him to warm up to me, so we could form some kind of bond. No one else in the entire house gave a fuck about me. But for some reason this guy seemed like he had a heart. Whether he knew it or not, he was going to be my ticket out of there.

Before he could tell me what his daughter's name was, we were both startled when someone knocked on the front door. He looked at me like he'd seen a fucking ghost. I looked back at him and said nothing. I thought he was going to get up and see who it was, but he didn't move.

The knocking didn't stop, so he pressed the mute button on the remote, got up, and tiptoed down the hallway. Before he left the room, he instructed me not to say a word. One part of me wanted to tell him to kiss my ass, but the other part of me wanted to honor his wish. He was being nice to me, and I didn't want to ruin the progress we'd made so far.

The person at the front door continued to knock, but Breon refused to answer the door. Several seconds later, he tiptoed back into the room. He looked at me in a very weird way and then he took a seat.

Curiosity was burning inside me. "Who's knocking at the door?" I asked.

"It's Dré's baby's mama."

"Why didn't you tell her he was gone?"

"Because she looked like she already had an attitude, so I knew she wouldn't believe me."

When the knocking stopped, he said, "Good. She's gone."

Hearing him say she was gone almost gave me a nervous breakdown. If I had gotten up the courage to yell, she probably would've thought Dré was in here and tried to break down the door to see what was going on. Now my chances of using her were gone.

Breon turned the volume back up on the television and continued to watch.

I sat there with an expression of disgust on my face. I was devastated, and there wasn't a thing I could do about it. With nothing else to do, I tuned back in to *The First 48*.

After five minutes or so of watching TV, we were startled again by loud knocking. This time it came from the back window. When I heard it, I knew without a doubt that it was that same chick. She had walked to the back of the house and started banging on the window of the room where we sat.

She yelled, "Dré, I know you're in there, you no good motherfucker! Let me in before I break this damn window!"

Breon stood and looked at me. He placed his finger up to his mouth to tell me not to say a word.

"I see somebody in there! Dré, I know it's your ass! Open up the door and let me in there!"

"Help! They got me tied up in here!" I screamed. "Help me! Heeeeeellll—," I tried to say once more, but was silenced by a hard blow to the back of my head, and then everything around me went dark.

TURNING BACK
THE CLOCK

When I regained consciousness, I immediately felt a horrible pain at the back of my head. My head was pounding uncontrollably. It felt like I had been hit with a heavy piece of metal. I didn't have to touch the back of my head to know I had a great big lump back there. When I opened my eyes, I realized that my mouth was taped shut again, and Breon was standing within a couple feet of me. He didn't look too happy, so I knew he wasn't going to be nice to me anymore. I don't know what happened to that chick, or how he'd handled the situation, but she was gone, and I was still here, so that said a lot.

My head continued to ache. The pain was so excruciating, I almost started crying. I needed something to make the pain go away, but I knew Breon wasn't about give me any headache medicine. I just had to sit there and endure it.

After about an hour and a half, I heard voices coming through the front door. Breon jumped to his feet and greeted the people in the hallway. My heart started pounding all over again. I couldn't tell what was hurting more between my head and my heart, because both of them were getting to me.

"Where is L.L.?" I heard Breon ask.

"He had to make another run, but he'll be back soon," Dré said.

I heard Breon let out a loud sigh. I knew he was about to bring them up to speed about what had happened while they were gone. I really didn't want him to tell them what I did, but I knew it was bound to happen. I was just glad my uncle wasn't here to hear it. I knew he'd be very angry and would try to hurt me really badly.

"I had to knock that bitch out in there," I heard him say.

"Why? What she do?" Dré asked.

"Yeah, what she do?" Kasey chimed in.

"Trice came over here and started knocking on the front door real loud, but I didn't answer it. So she went to the back of the house and started banging on the window in the room where we got homegirl. I ain't gon' lie, the shit scared the hell out of me, because I thought she was gone. But when she started banging on the window in the back, she started yelling through the glass saying, "I see somebody in there! Dré, I know it's your ass! Open up the door and let me in there before I bust this fucking window open.' And before I could do anything, that bitch in there started yelling like a madwoman, saying, 'Help! They got me tied up in here. Help!'"

"You bullshitting me!" Dré said.

"Nah, I ain't. So right when she was about to scream again, I punched her right in the back of her fucking head and knocked her ass out."

"That bitch is crazy!" I heard Kasey blurt out. "I knew L.L. should've let me stay here, because none of that shit would've happened."

"Did Trice hear her?" Dré asked.

"Yeah, she heard her. But right after I knocked her out, I drug her ass out of the room and hid her in the hall closet, and then I let Trice in."

"What she say?" Dré asked.

"She was like, 'Who was that bitch I heard screaming? I know y'all got some ho up in here.'"

"And whatcha tell her?"

"I told her that was the TV she heard, and that you and Kasey went uptown to meet somebody."

"Did she believe you?" Dré asked.

"She didn't have a choice."

"I'm surprised she didn't try to look in closets and shit," Dré said, and then I heard him chuckle.

"She did. She ran right upstairs and looked in all the bedrooms and the closets. I guess she thought that if you had a bitch hiding in here she would've been upstairs, because she didn't look in any of the closets down here. After she came back downstairs, she walked right out the front door. I just stood there and watched her leave."

Now I heard footsteps coming my way. I knew that in a couple minutes all three of them would be staring in my face and making little comments about my actions. I really didn't care at this point, because if they were in my shoes, they would have done the exact same thing, if not more.

When all three of them made it into the room where I was, they cut their conversation short. All eyes were on me.

Kasey walked right up to me and said, "I heard you were showing off, Ms. Bad Ass! I know one thing, if I was here, I would've done more than knock your ass out. I would've tortured your silly ass."

Dré didn't say one word. He just looked at me and shook his head like he was disappointed in me, or like what I did was a shame. But that shit went right over my head. I really wasn't concerned about any of these frauds. My main focus was my uncle; he held the key to my life. Whatever they had to say to me didn't hold any merit. It went through one ear and out the next.

"When did you tape her mouth back up?" Dré asked Breon after they both took a seat on the sofa.

"Right after I knocked her stupid ass out. I wasn't about to let her wake up and start asking me a whole lot of fucking questions again. Or start apologizing about what she did. I wasn't in the mood to hear her mouth anymore."

Dré laughed. "Boy, I would've paid anything to see when you punched her in the back of her head. I bet that shit was funny as hell!"

"It wasn't funny at the time. I was madder than a motherfucker!"

Dré chuckled again. "I bet you was!" He looked over at me and smiled.

Personally I didn't see a motherfucking thing to smile

about. I was tied up and bound to a fucking chair. And on top of that, my fucking head was in severe pain. So what the fuck was his problem? Then we had Ms. Ride-or-Die chick standing alongside these two idiots, like she was fucking G.I. Jane or somebody. With all the anger and hostility I'd had buried inside me, I'd fuck her up on a good day.

I sat there and watched all three of these clowns while they entertained each other. I noticed Kasey didn't have any class whatsoever. She went into the kitchen refrigerator and got a forty-ounce bottle of beer. When she walked back into the room, she had the bottle tilted up to her mouth. She was literally drinking from the bottle. That was some shit you saw cats in the streets do.

After she took a couple sips of the beer, she passed the bottle to Dré, and then Dré passed it to Breon. Once the bottle was empty, Kasey started playing with it. She placed both hands around the neck of the bottle and had the bottom of it pressed against her pelvic area, like she was holding a penis of some kind.

Dré and Breon thought it was hilarious. Especially when the dumb bitch walked over to me, grabbed me by the back of my head, and pulled my head forward, while she used her other hand to hold on to the bottle. She acted like she had a dick and I was about to suck it. I was furious with this dumb chick.

Breon and Dré laughed so hard, they started choking. It seemed like the more Kasey played her sick game, the harder they laughed.

"Take off the tape and make her suck on it for real," Dré suggested.

"Nah, don't take the tape off," Breon said. "The bitch might scream again."

Kasey said, "I wish she would scream. I'll punch her right in her fucking mouth."

Dré stood. "Untie her legs and take her out the chair."

Kasey turned around toward Dré. "Whatcha gon' do?"

Dré walked toward me and grabbed my legs. "Help me untie her," he instructed Kasey.

Kasey got down on her knees, while I watched Dré untie my legs. I had no idea what they were about to do with me, but believe me, I was anxious to find out.

I sat there and went along with their fucking games. Dré instructed Kasey to help him put me down on the floor and flip me over on my stomach. They had caught me completely off guard. While they were trying to turn me over on my stomach, I started wiggling and kicking my legs frantically.

"Hold her legs," Dré told Kasey.

"The stupid bitch keeps moving."

"Yo, Breon, come hold her head down while me and Kasey hold her legs."

"What y'all 'bout to do?" he asked as he stood from the sofa. He hesitated for a second, and then he moved toward us in slow motion. I could tell he didn't want to be a part of what Dré and Kasey had going on. His facial expression told it all.

"Come on, nigga, grab her head and hold it down,"

Dré told him.

Breon kneeled on the floor, turned my head in the opposite direction to face the wall, and then he pressed both of his hands down on my head. The weight of his arms and hands was enough pressure to cave my head in. I already had a headache from when he'd punched me in the back of my head, so now I was experiencing such excruciating pain, I thought I might black out again.

While Breon held my head, Dré held my legs.

The next thing I know, Kasey had ripped off my pantyhose and panties, and she jammed the top of the beer into my vagina. I screamed and cried out as loud as I could, but no one could hear me because my mouth was still duct-taped. Tears poured from my eyes like a river.

She pulled the bottle out and rammed it back inside me again. She did it over and over again until I lost count of how many times I was violated. I couldn't see anyone's facial expressions, but I heard Breon telling them that they needed to stop.

Kasey chuckled. "Nigga, stop being a pussy!"

"You know I ain't no pussy! But I do know I ain't trying to be a part of this shit!"

Dré laughed. "Come on, nigga, calm your ass down! This shit ain't funny to you?"

"Hell, nah, this shit ain't funny!" Breon released my head.

I couldn't see what he was doing, but I knew he stood because he grunted as he scrambled to get on his feet. I couldn't lift my head for all the money in the world. I was sore, and my head was pounding. All I wanted was for someone to rescue me from all this madness. I hadn't done anything to deserve this type of abuse. I didn't even know these people, so why were they taking me through all this unnecessary torture?

Right after Breon released my head and got up, Kasey ceased all her activity. She pulled the bottle from my vagina and sat it on top of the coffee table next to the sofa. After she stood, Dré released my legs and also stood.

I lay there and cried. The way Kasey had forced that bottle inside me led me to believe that blood was everywhere. I thought they were going to pick me up and place me back in the chair, but they left me lying there on the floor. Even though my hands were still tied behind my back, my legs were untied. If I had just one ounce of will power, I could have jumped to my feet and hauled ass out of there. I would have run headfirst into the first window I saw—Fuck going out the front door! But I had no energy to move even an inch.

I don't know how much time passed, but it felt like I was lying on the floor forever. At first I thought they were going to leave me down there until my uncle got back, but then Breon stood, grabbed me by my arms, and instructed me to put my weight on him. I knew then that he was going to put me back into the chair.

"Dré, go upstairs and get her a wet washcloth," Breon told him.

"Ain't no clean washcloths upstairs," Dré said.

"Come on, there's gotta be something we can wipe her off with."

"Breon, you act like we fucking live here," Kasey said. "Who has clean washcloths in a fucking stash house?"

"Dré, what did you wash with after you fucked Brenda the other night?"

Dré laughed. "I used toilet paper."

"What did Brenda use?"

"She used toilet paper too. And then she carried her ass home."

Breon shook his head. "Man, we can't leave her looking like this. L.L. ain't gon' be happy when he come back here and find her like this."

"You think he gon' say something about a bitch who probably had his daughter killed?" Kasey asked. "L.L. don't give a fuck about her! Because if he did, he wouldn't have choked her ass out like he did earlier."

"Look, I don't care what y'all say. We need to find something to get this shit up with. I'm not gonna be walking 'round here with blood all on the motherfucking floor, like that shit looks good. I mean, come on. If the police happened to run up in here because they thought we had some dope up in here and saw her like this, all our asses is going to jail. And I ain't trying to go to jail behind this dumb-ass shit Kasey did."

"I ain't the only one who had a part in it!" she snapped. "It was Dré's idea."

"So what! You shoved the bottle in her pussy, not me."

I sat there and watched all three of these losers go back and forth about who did what, knowing they all had a hand in sexually assaulting me. I was the fucking victim, not them, so they all needed to shut the fuck up.

Finally Breon came up with the idea of how he was going to clean up the mess they'd made. He instructed Kasey to run to the corner store to get a bar of soap, a cotton cloth of some kind, bleach, Brillo Pads, and carpet cleaner. After she left, he picked up my panties and pantyhose and threw them in the trash.

I sat there in the chair with teary, red eyes. When he looked at me, I knew he could see all the hurt I was feeling. I could tell by his expression that what he and the rest of his crew had done to me was fucking with his conscience. He didn't apologize to me, but he looked like he was sorry.

Since it was Dré's idea to assault me, Breon instructed him to clean the blood off the floor when Kasey came back with the supplies. Dré used the carpet cleaner and the bleach to scrub my blood out of the carpet. He also instructed Kasey to lather the dish towel with the soap she'd bought from the store. The towel was thick enough to use as an oven mitten, but in this case she used it to clean my vagina.

I didn't want this bitch to touch me, but if I wanted to be clean, she was the one to do it. I watched her as she wiped off my thigh area, and the blood from the area around my vagina. I felt really awkward because of how she looked at me. The way she moved the cloth back and forth around my thighs and my vagina, it was like she enjoyed looking at me. I felt like I was being violated all over again.

When she finally finished wiping me down, she disposed of the cloth in the trash. I was left sitting on the chair feeling totally degraded. I never knew how it felt to be raped, but now I did.

TURNING
UP THE HEAT

Not too long after I was tied in the chair again, Dré's phone rang. His conversation didn't last very long. Immediately after he hung up, he looked at Breon and Kasey and told them that my uncle would be there in less than an hour.

"What's the holdup?" Breon asked.

"He said he was waiting for the nigga to come pick up the shit he had for 'em."

"Come on now, dog! It don't take that long to get rid of a couple of flat-screen TVs."

"He told me the nigga Ray Ray was short on the cash, so he made him go back to the crib and get the rest of his dough."

"That's some bullshit! He knew I had shit to do!"

"Well, go handle your business."

"I ain't leaving until I get my money from his ass."

"Well, then chill out," Dré said, a smirk on his face.

Breon threw his hands in the air. "Man, whatever! I don't even give a fuck." He walked out of the room.

Dré and Kasey both laughed at Breon after he left.

"Did you see that nigga's face? He was pissed off," Kasey said.

"He ain't really pissed off about the money. He's mad because his girl told him to be home an hour ago to get the kids while she went to work."

"Shit! He's flipping on us like it's our fault."

"Don't take it personal. You know how he acts when shit ain't going his way. He'll be a'ight when L.L. gets here and hands him his paper," Dré said.

I can't tell you where Breon went, but I knew he went outside. Dré and Kasey eventually stopped talking about Breon and jumped to another subject.

My head was still throbbing, and my vagina was having its own episode. For the life of me, I couldn't collect my thoughts. I tried praying to God a couple of times, but as soon as I got halfway through the prayer, my mind went blank.

Kasey also threw off my train of thought when she started talking about one particular chick on the rap video. She disgusted the hell out of me when she talked about how fat this chick's ass was. Dré sat back and laughed with her like they were both sitting in the front row of a fucking comedy show.

It didn't take long for Breon to come back into the house. I assumed he just went outside to catch some fresh air, since he hadn't done so while he was in the house watching me. When he walked back into the room where we were, he took a seat on the sofa next to Kasey. Kasey looked at Dré, but neither one of them said a word to Breon, who sat there in complete silence the entire time. I could tell he was angry, and they knew it too.

I decided to block these assholes out of my head and think about Uncle Lanier. I knew he was on his way back, so my time was about to run out. There was no way I could tell him what his flunkies had done to me, and he'd actually do something about it, because I was on his shit list. I would be wasting my breath.

Some way or another, though, they needed to pay for what they'd done to me. Everyone, including my uncle, needed to suffer on some level. I had no idea how it would happen, but I knew it needed to be done.

Every child in the world had their own imaginary superhero, but I really needed one to rescue me now. Where the fuck was Superman when I needed him?

Tied up to a chair with my mouth duct-taped, all I could think about was where I'd gone wrong and how I'd ended up here. I believed that God existed. I was brought up in the church, so I knew He was real. But what I wanted to know was, *Where is He when I need Him the most?*

From the day I'd met Ricky, I thought my life had turned around for the better, but in all actuality, it had made a turn for the worse. All the expensive cars, the clothes, the money, and our beautiful home blinded me from seeing that I had fallen into a trap. From the moment I had a taste of the good life, it was hard for me to have anything less. After Ricky got killed, every man I'd affiliated myself with had plenty of money. And if I looked at the pattern, every last one of those cats had some type of baggage, so our relationship always fell to the wayside.

Unfortunately, my cousin Nikki followed in my footsteps, because I created an image in her mind. She was so blinded by all my possessions, she couldn't see the shit I had to go through to get them. In her twisted head, I was an idol. And because she wanted to walk in my shoes, she created a similar life, and it resulted in her own demise. Now I had to pay for her mistakes with my own life, which was really fucked up. If I had a choice to turn back the clock, I would've walked in the opposite direction when I saw Ricky coming my way, and then my life would've been drama-free. My grandmother would still be here, Quincy would still be here, and Nikki would still be here. Most importantly, I wouldn't be tied up in a stash house, praying that God would spare my life.

The pain in my head started subsiding, but my insides still throbbed with intense pain. I knew the only thing that would help ease the soreness was some type of narcotic. Not only would the narcotic numb my pain, but it might even help me to forget where I was.

As I was daydreaming about pain relief, I heard a loud knock on the door. My heart fell into the pit of my stomach. There was no doubt in my mind that it was Uncle Lanier. He had already called Dré and informed him that he was on his way, so it had to be him.

Kasey jumped to her feet and dashed to the front door. I looked at Dré and Breon, and they both looked back at me. I knew they saw the fear in my eyes because my pupils became enlarged, and sweat pellets poured from my forehead.

I heard the front door open, and then I heard a voice say, "Where is Breon?"

I couldn't believe it. It was a woman's voice asking for Breon. She sounded really upset, so I figured it had to be his baby's mama.

Kasey yelled, "Breon, Sabrina at the door."

"Oh, so you ain't gon' let me come in the house?"

"Nah, 'cause they handling some business back there."

Sabrina snapped. "When the fuck did y'all change the rules 'round here? Kasey, you know you been letting me come in the house when they handling business in the back!"

Kasey sighed. "I know, but it's really some heavy shit going on back there. And, plus, we got this new dude back there, and he's real paranoid about letting people in the house when he's here, so that's why I can't let you in."

Sabrina sucked her teeth. "What the fuck ever! I didn't want to come in this piece of shit anyway!"

Breon hopped up from the sofa and raced to the front door. If I had a chance to get her attention, I wouldn't care if these motherfuckers in here killed me afterward. Just knowing I took a chance to get out of this place would allow me to die peacefully.

When Breon got to the front door, I heard him say, "What's up, boo?"

"Why the fuck you ain't been home yet?" she screamed.

"You knew I had to be at work over an hour ago."

While Breon stood there and explained himself, Kasey brought her gay ass back in the room with me and Dré.

Dré looked at her and whispered, "I'm glad you didn't let that bitch walk in here."

"She tried to," she whispered back, "but I stuck my foot in the door and stopped her."

"Can you just give me about fifteen more minutes? The nigga I'm waiting on said he was on his way here."

"How the fuck you gon' tell me to give you fifteen more minutes when I'm already late for work? Them crackers in that nursing home already trying to fire my ass for all those other times I came in late, and now you telling me to give you a few more minutes. Fuck that, 'cause you sound real stupid!"

Then it got really quiet.

Next I heard some footsteps, and then I heard Breon say, "What the fuck you doing?"

Several seconds later, a child's voice asked, "Mommy, where you going?"

Then another child chimed in and asked the same question. The children sounded like they were at least four to five years old.

"Come on, Sabrina, you know you can't leave them here like that!" Breon yelled.

Kasey and Dré both jumped to their feet and rushed toward the front door to see what was going on.

Boy, this would've been a perfect time for me to escape. No one was in the room with me, so if I had enough strength to get my hands untied, I could've gotten the fuck out of there, and they wouldn't have been able to do shit about it. Unfortunately, all my strength and will was gone from the abuse I'd suffered.

"Yo, dog, they can't stay here," Dré said.

"Yeah, Breon. What the fuck is she doing?"

Breon ignored them both. He was more focused on trying to get Sabrina not to leave the kids with him. He must have known how detrimental it would be to those kids if they saw me bound and tied up.

"Fuck you, nigga! I gotta go to work! And I'm not gonna let you or anybody else get me fired!"

Shortly after that I heard a car door slam, and then I heard tires squeal as the car drove off.

Breon must've walked away from the house, because Dré and Kasey both were talking mad shit about him while his kids ran around on the front porch. I guess Dré and Kasey stood at the front door to keep them from running into the house.

Several minutes later, I heard Breon's voice again. "Man, I hate that bitch sometimes!"

"Whatcha gon' do with the kids? You know you can't bring 'em in here," Dré said.

"So what I'm gon' do with 'em? Leave 'em outside?" Breon asked.

"Come on now, dog. Don't ask me that!"

"Well, I'm telling you right now that I ain't gon' leave 'em outside!"

"Take 'em upstairs," Kasey suggested.

I was waiting for Breon to respond, but he didn't. All I heard was a clatter of footsteps going up the staircase.

Kasey and Dré marched their asses back in the room with me. As soon as they sat back down, they started running their mouths about Breon. Kasey thought it was funny that his baby's mama dropped off the kids at the front door and then bailed on Breon.

"She's stupid as hell!" Dré said. "I don't even know why he still puts up with her shit! I would've packed my shit a long time ago."

"I would've left her ass a long time ago too," Kasey said.

I sat back and listened to them bad-mouth Sabrina. They spoke in a low tone to prevent Breon from hearing them. I had only been here for a few hours, and I could tell that Breon was a different breed from Kasey and Dré. It seemed like these two leaned on each other, while Breon stood alone, because he had more backbone. I could also tell that they wouldn't stand up against him if a war ever broke out amongst them.

Dré and Kasey drowned themselves in the television, surfing through the channels, looking for rap videos. Then, when they got tired of that, Kasey persuaded Dré to stick in a porno DVD. Kasey sat back on the sofa, giddy as hell, when the movie started.

I was fucking disgusted. I would've puked on myself if I my mouth wasn't duct-taped. How dare they watch this bullshit in front of me? I felt violated all over again, especially after what they'd done to me.

While all the fucking and sucking was going on with these characters on this bootleg movie, I saw a shadow move through my peripheral vision. The shit scared the hell out of me, so I jumped and got the attention of Kasey and Dré.

"What the fuck!" Dré jumped to his feet.

I saw a little head and hand peer around the corner into the room where we were, and then the person vanished. I knew it was one of Breon's kids.

Dré caught the little kid before he or she could get away. "Yo, Bre!" Dré yelled when he got into the hallway.

"Yeah," I heard Breon reply, but it was very faint.

A little voice said, "He's in the bathroom."

"Yo, Damon, get your ass upstairs with your pops before I take my belt off," Dré threatened.

When I heard Dré chastise the child by his name, I knew it was a little boy who'd sneaked downstairs. I didn't get a good look at him, so I couldn't say how old he was, but I just hoped he had enough sense to go home and tell his mother what he'd seen.

"I told him not to go downstairs," a little girl said.

"Shut up and stop being a tattletale," Damon said as he marched upstairs.

"Get cha ass up here!" Breon roared.

"Yo, man, he came down here and peeped into the back room," Dré told him.

"Did he see homegirl?"

"Hell yeah, he saw her."

Smack!

"Oooowww! That hurts," Damon said.

"Nigga, get your ass in that fucking room, and don't you come out!" Breon growled.

Dré was pissed off, but he didn't dwell on it. All he said to Breon was that he needed to handle the situation.

"I got this," Breon said.

Dré didn't say another word. He walked back into the room where Kasey and I were and sat down.

Kasey asked, "How the fuck he let Damon get out the room?"

"He was in the bathroom, and Damon snuck out."

"You think he gon' tell his mama what he saw?"

"I don't know."

"Well, we can't take that chance," Kasey said. "As soon as L.L. gets back, he's gon' have to take her out of here."

"Where the fuck he gon' take her?"

"That ain't our motherfucking problem. We did our part. We knocked her out, tied her up, and held her until he got here. Now all the rest of that shit is on him."

"I know he ain't gon' be trying to move her out of here. It's gon' be too risky."

"So what the fuck was he gon' do with her anyway? I mean, he was gon' have to take her out of here eventually."

"Whatcha think Breon is here for?" Dré asked.

"I'm not following you."

Before Dré said another word, he hesitated and looked at me. I looked straight into his eyes and waited for him to explain himself, but when realized I was eavesdropping on their conversation, he tried to put a lid on it.

"Come here and let me holler at you for a minute," he told Kasey, and got up from the sofa. And they walked into the kitchen.

I strained myself to hear them, but it was impossible. I heard them whispering, but their words were indistinguishable. Whatever it was they didn't want me to hear had to be bad. I mean, what could be worse than what had already been done to me? Unless my uncle planned to kill me or have me killed. Knowing that could be a possibility scared the shit out of me. I didn't want to be killed. I wasn't ready to meet my Maker. I still had some things I wanted to do before I left this earth.

While they were in their huddle, someone knocked on the front door. My heart skipped a beat. This time I knew it was my uncle. He was the only one they'd been expecting to come here.

Dré strolled toward the front door, while Kasey walked back into the room with me.

Immediately after Dré opened the door, I heard my uncle say, "Man, you won't believe all the shit I had to deal with."

My heart started racing. Whatever his plans were for me, I knew he was about to carry them out. It became clear to me that his only purpose for keeping me alive was for me to tell him what had really happened to Nikki. Once he got me to spill the beans, I wouldn't be any good to him.

I heard both of their footsteps walking down the hallway. The closer they came to entering the room, the faster my heart pumped. I was filled with so many emotions, I couldn't think straight. I knew I was about to embark on yet another one of my uncle's grueling torture sessions.

When he turned the corner, he looked straight at me. Then his eyes drifted toward my legs. His eyes looked bloodshot, and his face menacing. Everything about him looked evil, so I became more terrified than before.

"Didn't she have on some stockings?" he asked.

Dré started stuttering. "Yeah-uh-uh, she had some on, but, uh-uh—"

"She had to use the bathroom," Kasey said. "She just didn't put 'em back on."

"Y'all took her to the bathroom?" he asked.

"Yeah," Kasey told him. "Why? I mean, was we not supposed to?"

"I would've made her piss on herself and see how she liked it."

"Nah, we didn't want to be that cruel," Kasey said. "Besides, we got bigger problems than that."

"What's the problem?" Lanier looked at Dré and Kasey.

"You gon' have to take her out of here," Dré said.

"Why the fuck I gotta take her out of here?" he roared. "I thought Breon was gonna handle it when I was done with her."

"That's how it was supposed to be. But Breon's baby's mama came by and dropped off her kids on the front porch and left, so Breon took 'em upstairs. But while he was in the bathroom, his son snuck downstairs and saw homegirl tied up. Now the li'l boy is six years old, so he's old enough to understand what the fuck is going on. But we're not sure if he's gonna go back and tell his mama what he saw."

My uncle's face turned red. "Where is Breon now?"

"Upstairs," Kasey said.

"Tell 'im to come downstairs, but make sure you tell 'im to leave his kids upstairs."

Kasey ran upstairs and returned with Breon several minutes later.

Breon looked like he wasn't in the mood for idle chitchat. "What's up?" he asked.

"Dré just told me your son snuck downstairs and saw Kira tied up, so now I'm gonna have to switch shit up and take her out of here."

"You ain't gotta take her out of here," Breon said.

"Why he don't?" Dré asked.

"Because my son ain't gon' say shit!"

"Breon, we can't take that chance," Dré said.

"So what the fuck you gon' do then?"

My uncle turned to look at Dré, who seemed to have all the answers. Dré stood there with a puzzled expression.

"How are we gonna get her out of here without anybody seeing her?" Lanier asked. "Because we aren't gonna be able to take her out the front door."

"We gon' have to knock her out cold, wrap her up in a blanket, and take her out through the back," Dré said.

"Everything you said sounded good up to the part

where we take her through the back," my uncle said. "How the hell are we going to get her in the trunk of the car, when there's no driveway that leads from the front of the house to the back?"

Everyone in the room fell silent.

"Fuck it! We gon' have to take her out the front door," Dré said.

"We can't take her out of here tied up with fucking tape across her mouth," Lanier said.

"I know that. We gon' have to let her walk out of here like she walked in here, but this time we gon' have to stick a burner in her back and let her know that if she opens her fucking mouth, we gon' put a hot one in her."

"That shit ain't gon' work!" Breon said. "You think she gives a fuck if one of us got a fucking burner in her back to shoot her if she opened her mouth? Man, wake the fuck up and smell the coffee. Look at what she's going through in here with us. You think she ain't gonna take the chance to scream for help if somebody was around?"

"He's right," Kasey said.

"I don't give a fuck who's right or wrong," Lanier said. "The fact of the matter is, the plan I had set up is now fucked up because of your son, Breon. And now I'm forced to figure out some other shit."

Breon said, "Yo, for real, homeboy, you can say what the fuck you wanna say, but my thing is this. If you'd handled your business with her first before leaving here to go get rid of some fucking hot-ass TVs, we wouldn't be going through this shit!"

Lanier gritted his teeth. "Nigga, what I do ain't none of your motherfucking business! So you need to watch what the fuck you say out your motherfucking mouth."

Breon took two steps toward Lanier. I knew Breon was trying to intimidate him. He stood at least three inches taller than him, and he was every bit of forty-five pounds heavier. Standing next to each other, my uncle looked like P. Diddy, and Breon looked like Rick Ross.

"Nah, nigga, you need to watch what the fuck comes out your mouth!"

Kasey and Dré both looked at each other, but before either one of them could say anything, Lanier reached his hand underneath the back of his shirt and pulled out a pistol. My eyes grew huge.

Dré got between them before he raised it and got a chance to point it toward Breon. "Yo, y'all need to go ahead with this bullshit, 'cause this ain't gon' solve a damn thing."

"Nigga, I know you ain't pulled your pistol out on me!" Breon tried to push Dré out of the way.

Kasey looked like she wanted to run, but she stood there with a dumbfounded expression and said nothing.

Again I wished I wasn't tied up, because this would have been the perfect opportunity to escape. With all the commotion going on, they wouldn't have noticed that I was gone. But since I was strapped down and stuck smack-dab in the middle of this crap, I just sat there and prayed that if any bullets were shot off, I wouldn't get hit.

Between the pushing and the shoving, Lanier managed to keep his gun pointed toward the floor. I didn't think he had any intentions of pulling the trigger. He just wanted to prove to Breon that he wasn't afraid of him.

Breon ended up leaving the room, but before he stormed out, he looked at my uncle and said, "You're a lucky nigga!"

"Nah, nigga, you're the lucky one!" Lanier yelled back. Once he heard Breon walking back upstairs, he stuck his gun back under his shirt.

Kasey sighed heavily and took a seat back on the sofa.

Dré stood in front of my uncle with his hands pressed against his chest. "Come on, dog," he said. "Leave that shit alone. It ain't even worth it."

"Help me untie her," Lanier told Dré.

"Whatcha gon' do?" Dré asked.

"I'm gonna take her out of here."

"How you gon' get her to the car?"

"I'm gonna back my car up on the grass alongside the house as far as my car will let me, and you gon' bring her out the back."

Kasey asked. "You sure that's gon' work?"

"It's gonna have to," my uncle told her.

It didn't take them long to untie me. My legs were so numb, I couldn't stand up without their help. A few seconds after I stood with the help of Dré and my uncle standing on each side of me, I heard three sets of footsteps marching down the staircase. I immediately knew it was Breon and his children coming downstairs.

Dré looked at Kasey. "Go see what the fuck he's doing."

Kasey ran to the entrance of the hallway. I heard her ask Breon what he was about to do.

"I'm getting my motherfucking kids out of here before they witness me do some damage around this motherfucker!"

"You taking them home?" she asked.

"Nah, I'm taking them up the block to their aunt's house."

Kasey looked back at Dré.

"A'ight," Dré replied. "Let 'im go on out the door, so the kids won't see homegirl,"

I heard the front door open and close before Kasey could even give Dré's instructions to Breon. Now that the kids were gone, Dré and my uncle moved quickly toward the hallway.

When they got me into the hallway, Lanier told Kasey to grab my purse off the table, hang it around my neck, and then switch places with him. Then he added, "Help Dré take her outside, while I get my car and back it up to the side of the house."

Kasey did as he told her, and as soon as he walked out the front door, they made a right into the kitchen and escorted me to the back door. Even though my legs weren't tied up, my wrists were still tied together, and my mouth was still duct-taped, so I didn't see any possibility of escaping.

COMBAT MISSION

On my way through the kitchen, I got a chance to see the clock on the wall, and I saw that it was a few minutes after nine o'clock. There were no lights on in the back of the house, so it was totally dark outside and spooky-looking.

Kasey asked Dré, "You think we should turn on the back porch light?"

"Hell, nah, because somebody from the house on the other side of the fence might see us dragging her to the car with fucking tape all over her mouth. So let's just take her down the back stairs and wait for L.L. to walk around the side to meet us."

Kasey sighed. "Yeah, a'ight."

It didn't take my uncle long to back up his car on the grass beside the old, wretched-ass house. A couple seconds later, I heard a car door slam, and then I heard someone coming toward us.

"Hey, where y'all at?" Lanier asked in a low whisper.

Dré spoke up. "We're standing at the bottom of the stairs."

"I can't see you, so walk toward the corner of the house."

"A'ight."

Dré and Kasey stepped forward, and then they yanked me to get me to the corner of the house. When we got to the edge of the house, we saw my uncle's brake lights as he backed up his car. After he put his car in park, he jumped out of the driver's seat to help them load me into his car. I had no idea if he planned to put me in the backseat or stuff me in the trunk, but I was soon to find out.

"Come on, bring her to the car," he told them.

"A'ight, we coming." Dré began to drag me through the grass once more.

"Are we gonna put her in the trunk or what?" Kasey asked.

"Yeah. Give me a minute to press the trunk button."

My heart sank into the pit of my stomach. I didn't want to be thrown in the back of a trunk. I wasn't some load of trash for him to dump into the nearest dumpster. I was precious cargo, and someone needed to recognize that.

Kasey and Dré escorted me to the back of my uncle's car. They stood there patiently and waited for him to hit the button to unlock the trunk.

"What's the holdup?" Dré asked.

"I can't see the fucking button."

"Ain't it right there underneath your steering wheel?"

"That's where I'm feeling."

While he searched for the button that controlled the trunk, I looked toward the sky and prayed to God that someone would come by and help me escape. I promised Him that I would turn my life over to Him if He allowed me to get out of this rut. I knew I couldn't do it by myself, so if He'd just send someone to my rescue, I would forever be in His debt.

Before I ended my prayer, my attention was diverted by a loud gunshot, which scared the hell out of me. When I looked in the direction where that single shot came, I saw the silhouette of someone running toward us.

The bullet shattered the windshield of my uncle's car and penetrated one of the front seats. Lanier immediately took cover and dove to the ground, and Kasey and Dré released my arms and ran back into the house, leaving me standing there all alone. Without thinking twice, I ducked down behind the back of the car.

"Don't hide now, motherfucker! Get back up!" I heard the gunman roar.

My uncle didn't respond. I assumed he knew it was Breon, because I knew it was him the moment he spoke.

My uncle returned fire, letting off four rounds. It sounded like a cannon, but I couldn't tell if Breon got hit or dove down to the ground. I couldn't see shit. I did hear my uncle crawling, and it sounded like he was coming around the other side of the car where I was. I was sure he didn't know Dré and Kasey had left me out here all alone. It was too dark for him to see anything. Shit, I could barely see what was around me, but my ears were working overtime. The closer he came to me, the farther I moved in the opposite direction.

While I squatted and crab-walked, I managed to get away from the car and get back to the back of the house.

When I looked up at the back door, I saw it was closed. I figured Dré or Kasey must have closed it immediately after they ran into the house.

While I moved around the back of the house, I heard more shots being fired. It sounded like the Fourth of July. The way I saw it, Breon wanted to see some bloodshed, and he wasn't going to stop until he got what he wanted.

He yelled, "Whatcha hiding for? You bitch-ass nigga!"

But my uncle still wouldn't respond. I couldn't tell if he had been hit, because I was too far away to hear any movement.

By this time I had reached the other side of the house. There was another old house that was at least sixty feet away. All the lights in that rundown shack were off, but I noticed a little bit of movement behind the curtains of one of the downstairs windows. You didn't have to be a rocket scientist to know that someone was in there trying to see who was doing the shooting. I started to approach the window to get that person's attention, but I decided against it when I realized that nobody was going to open their door after they'd heard gunshots. Every human being knew that was a no-no, so I kept moving.

Instead of heading toward the front of the house, I stayed in the back and moved from one backyard to the next. I thought I heard my uncle running behind me at one point, but when I ducked down behind a tall garbage can and waited a few minutes, I realized that it was just a stray cat. I let out a big sigh of relief.

After I sat there for a few moments, I noticed that all the gunshots had stopped. I couldn't tell who got shot or what was the outcome of it all, because I didn't stick around to see. My main concern was to get Kira to a safe place. So I stood and ran until I couldn't run anymore.

When I got to the last house on the block, I rushed across the street to the next block and dipped down into the alley behind a row of houses. The alley was dark and narrow, but I didn't care. This was my only way of escape, so I took it.

Not once did I look back. I figured that if those motherfuckers were looking for me, they were searching around the house, or maybe the neighbor's backyard. I knew they wouldn't think that I'd gotten very far, but I showed them.

REGAINING CONTROL

I knew I ran every bit of one mile to another neighborhood called Young's Park before I ran out of breath. I knew if my uncle or any one of the others was looking for me, they wouldn't have come looking over in this neighborhood. I thanked God that I had on some flat ballet shoes, because I wouldn't have made it this far in three- or four-inch heels.

As I got deeper into this neighborhood, I started seeing more streetlights. It was the projects, for Christ's sake, so everybody and their mother was standing outside. I did have a few enemies out here from my past. Ricky had fucked a couple chicks out here, so they hated my guts after he broke it off with them. I definitely didn't want any of them to see me tied up like this, so I dipped back around a black Dodge Magnum and ran up Virginia Beach Boulevard toward downtown Norfolk.

As I was ducking behind cars, I saw a car like my uncle's traveling in my direction. I quickly ducked behind a black Range Rover.

Suddenly the passenger window of the Rover rolled down, and a guy asked, "You a'ight?"

I didn't know whether I should run or just faint, because he startled the hell out of me. When I looked up and saw that he seemed genuinely concerned, a tear rolled down my face.

He stepped out of the car and immediately removed the duct tape from my mouth. It was a fucking relief to be able to move my mouth again. Without even asking me, he stuck his head back into the car, grabbed a box cutter from the glove compartment, and cut the rope off my wrists.

"Come on, take a seat in the car," he told me.

I was somewhat hesitant at first, but I figured since he'd untied me and took off the duct tape, he couldn't possibly want to hurt me. So I sat down in the backseat with the car door still ajar and my legs stretched out, letting my feet touch the ground. He stood in front of me and started asking me a thousand questions. My head was spinning, and I didn't know if I was coming or going. But something inside me told me that I was safe, and that it was OK to talk.

The guy asked me my name, who I was running from, and why they had me tied up. While I gathered my thoughts, I looked at him from head to toe. He was indeed a big guy, but he seemed like he was nice. He was light-skinned with long sideburns that connected to his beard. I figured he couldn't be older than thirty-five. When he smiled at me and told me that I was all right, and that no one else was going to hurt me, I believed him.

"Are you gonna tell me your name?" he asked again.

I took a deep breath and told him my name was Kira. When he realized I was beginning to open up to him, he stooped down in front of me and told me his name was Jamon, but everybody called him Fro. I tried to smile back at him, but I couldn't. Every joint in my body ached, and I felt like I was about to fall apart.

"Are you gonna tell me who you were running from?"

"I know this might sound crazy, but I was running from my uncle because he was trying to kill me."

"Nah, shorty, that shit don't sound crazy at all! I hear about that shit happening every day in my world."

"Well, I've never heard of or seen that type of shit before. That's why I'm kind of fucked-up in the head right now."

"Do you mind if I ask you why he was trying to kill you?"

"He thinks I know or had something to do with his daughter getting killed."

Fro looked at me with uncertainty. "Well, did you?"

"Of course, I didn't."

"Where is he now?"

"I'm not sure."

"So how did you get away?"

"It's a long story. And I don't feel like going back over it." I buried my face in my hands.

"So whatcha gon' do? I mean, do you live around here somewhere?"

"No. I don't live in VA anymore."

"Do you have other family or a homegirl that lives around here?"

"No."

"Well, do you wanna call the police?"

"Call them and say what?" Tears started falling from my eyes. "After all that shit I went through today, going to the police and having them arrest those motherfuckers wouldn't be enough for me. I wanna see every last one of those bastards go through some pain like I did."

"Well, damn! How many of them was it?"

"It was four of them at the house, but one of them, I could tell, really didn't want to take part in all that shit. So it's really three of them" I paused to collect my thoughts. "Oh yeah, I can't forget the motherfucker who set me up. He needs to get it too."

I waited for Fro to comment, but he just stood there in silence. I looked at him. "What's wrong? What? You ran out of questions?"

He gave me a half-smile. "Nah, I'm just standing here bugging out, trying to figure out how you should really handle this situation. I mean, it's just you. And you going up against four people ain't a good idea, especially since you ain't got no burner."

"Can you get me one?"

He chuckled. "Yo, Kira, you are really tripping right now. I think you need to sit back and analyze your situation before you fuck around and get into some shit you ain't gon' be able to get out of. I mean, it's a dog-eat-dog world out here, and niggas damn sure ain't playing fair."

"Look, Fro, I understand everything you're saying, but I have been sexually assaulted with a fucking beer bottle. I've got two knots in the back of my head from being hit with a heavy metal object. I've been punched in the face at least five times. And I was choked so badly, I almost lost consciousness."

Fro threw up his hands. "Damn, shorty, my bad. I didn't know it was like that."

"You telling me you don't see these fucking cuts and bruises on my face?"

"I saw 'em when you first came up to the car, but I thought maybe your man beat you up."

"Nah, this shit ain't come from no man of mine. This shit came from some cowards, and I'm going to make sure they pay for all the shit they took me through." I then began to cry uncontrollably.

Fro reached back inside the glove compartment, but this time he grabbed a handful of McDonald's napkins and handed them to me.

I wiped my eyes, but the tears kept falling. I had prayed to God to get me out of that situation, and He did. But somehow it felt like I was still there. I wasn't there physically, but I was still there mentally, so my captors still had the control.

"Yo, Kira, it's gonna be a'ight."

"I know it is," I told him as I continued to wipe the tears from my face.

While Fro and I tried to figure out what my next step would be, this tall, brown-skinned cat with a bunch of flashy jewelry walked up to us.

Fro immediately introduced him to me. "Eh, yo, Kira, this is my homeboy, Jay One."

Jay One leaned toward me and extended his hand. "Nice to meet you," he said.

I extended my head and nodded. Without asking my permission, Fro immediately brought Jay One up to speed about how I'd stumbled across him and why I looked so messed up. As Fro reiterated everything I'd told him, I could see sadness overtake Jay One.

Jay One looked down at me. "Damn! You went through all that?"

I didn't respond. I just looked at him and continued to wipe the tears from my face.

He looked back at Fro. "So, where she live at?"

"She said she used to live here, but now she lives out of town."

"Does she have any more family around here?"

"She said she didn't."

"So why is she here?" Jay One looked at me and back at Fro.

"I flew here from Houston because my cousin's funeral was earlier today."

"What was your cousin's name?" Jay One asked.

"Nikki."

He thought for a second. "Oh, nah, I don't know her."

"She got shot in Houston, so my uncle had her body shipped back here so he could bury her."

"How old was she?" Jay One asked.

"She was twenty-five."

Fro blurted out, "Damn! She was young as hell!"

"Yeah, she sho was," Jay One said.

Hearing both of the guys comment on how young Nikki was made me think about how soon her life was cut short. This was the first time I'd looked at it like that. I figured my uncle probably saw it that way as well. But she was a backstabber, a chick who couldn't be trusted. And when that cat she was fucking with named Bintu' saw that, he felt the need to eliminate her. So it wasn't my doing. Sadly I knew even if I had a chance to explain that to my uncle, he still wouldn't have believed me. End of story.

My train of thought was interrupted when Fro asked me if there was anywhere I needed him to take me. I thought about telling them to drop me off at my hotel, but something told me that going back there wouldn't be a good idea, because either Tony or my uncle would probably come there looking for me. I needed to go to another hotel, but first I needed to get my rental car.

I told Fro, "I need to get my rental car."

"Where is it?" Fro asked.

"I left it parked outside of the guy's house who set me up."

Fro and Jay One looked at each other then at me.

Fro said, "Yo, shorty, you might wanna leave that joint where it is."

"Yeah, he's right 'cause if homeboy knows that you got away from ol' dude, then they're probably waiting in the cut for you to show up."

"So what do you think I should do?" I asked, looking at both of them.

Fro shrugged, and Jay One pretty much did the same thing, remaining silent.

I sighed heavily. "Well, can one of y'all at least help me get a burner?"

Jay One looked at Fro. "Yo, cuz, you gon' have to help her with that one."

"Yo, shorty, do you even know how to handle a burner?"

"Of course."

"How much dough you got?" Fro asked.

"How much is it going to cost me?"

"It all depends on what you want."

"Can you get me a thirty-eight?"

Fro thought for a moment. "Yeah, I can do that."

"For how much?"

"Give me two big faces, and it's yours."

"What's big faces?" I asked. This was new VA slang, I guess.

Fro smiled. "Hundred-dollar bills, shorty."

"Oh, OK. I can swing that. But the gun ain't gonna be dirty, is it?"

"What do you care? You gon' use it and get rid of it anyway, right?"

"Yes, but I just don't want to be walking around with a gun with bodies on it."

"Yo, Kira, it ain't too many burners 'round here that ain't got a body on them," Fro said. "And if you find one, believe me, that joint gon' run you anywhere between five to eight hundred."

"Yeah, he ain't lying 'bout that, shorty."

"All right. I really don't care. Just get me something now. I'm running out of time."

"A'ight, let's get it then." Fro hopped back into the passenger seat.

Jay One got in on the driver's side, and after Fro told him where to drive, he put the car in gear, and we were off. I got him to stop by an ATM machine, so I could get the cash for the gun.

I knew the Tidewater area like the back of my hand. When Jay One traveled down Virginia Beach Boulevard, made a left onto Tidewater Drive, a right onto Princess Anne Road, and then an immediate left onto Reservoir Avenue, I knew he was going to Walt's place.

Walt was an old-timer who had lived on Reservoir Avenue forever. Everybody around town knew this cat, and anyone who needed a burner came to him. He had new pistols and used pistols. I knew he made a killing off burners. I remember hearing Ricky tell me one day that Walt had to be worth at least a couple million, and yet he lived in an old-ass house and drove an old 1995 Lincoln Continental. As long as I'd known Walt, he was never flashy, which was why I believed he had longevity on these streets. I knew seeing me again was going to blow his mind.

After we pulled up to Walt's house, Fro hopped out and asked me to hand him my money. Before I handed it to him, I asked him if we were at Mr. Walt's house.

Fro looked at me, clearly puzzled. "How the fuck you know Walt?"

"Well, if this is the same guy, I've known him since I was a little girl. My mother used to fuck with him back in the day."

"Damn, if this ain't a small-ass world!" Fro said.

I gave him a half-smile. "Tell me about it."

"What's your mama's name?" Fro asked. "I might remember her."

"Nah, you ain't gonna remember her. She's been deceased now for about twelve years. And, besides, when she was fucking with Mr. Walt, I think I was about ten years old. I used to call him Poppa Walt. And when he and my mother broke up, I didn't see him again until after my mother passed away."

"Well, since you already know him, let's go." Fro pulled on the door handle to let me out.

I got out of the truck. I had mixed feelings about seeing Walt. It had been a few years since I'd last seen him. I had introduced him to Ricky, and they'd done a little business together. While Walt supplied Ricky with the arsenal he needed, Ricky, in turn, greased Walt's palms. I knew Walt made at least ten grand from this deal with Ricky. But what I didn't know was whether Walt knew about our fed case. And, if he did, was he aware that I'd testified against Ricky and the rest of his crew? If he was, that wouldn't be a good look at all.

I'd known this man half of my life, so I knew he hated snitches. The reason why he survived on these streets and had longevity was because he stuck to a very important street code, meaning, he only fucked with legit people. Cats had to bring references with them when they needed something from Walt. At least four to five people had to vouch for his buyers before he did any business with them. He was a very thorough cat, and nothing got past him.

Fro walked ahead of me and went straight to Walt's back door. All the lights were off in the house, so I wondered if he was home. Seconds after Fro knocked on the door, it opened. He smiled when Walt made himself visible.

"You know what time it is, old-timer, so let a nigga in."

Walt smiled as he unlocked the screen door and pushed it open. Fro stepped into the house, and I followed. As I entered through the back door, I held my head down.

Walt grabbed me by the arm. "Do I know you?"

I was embarrassed to look into his face, but I did it anyway. I tried to smile, but my mood didn't allow me to do so.

Fro looked back at Walt. "She said she knew you. That's why she got out of the truck."

Walt pulled me closer and looked directly into my face. "Kira."

I tried to smile again, but the hurt and pain I had experienced not even two hours ago started weighing heavily on me. I didn't want him to see me cry, because I didn't feel like explaining to him what had happened to me. I didn't think he would understand, or even believe me.

Walt closed the door behind us and had me take a seat. He took a seat beside me and started asking a hundred and one questions. My eyes immediately got watery all over again.

"What happened to you? Who did this?"

When I didn't answer right away, he looked at Fro.

Fro shrugged as if to say he didn't know anything. Basically, Fro wanted me to do all the explaining.

Walt asked Fro, "Where'd you pick her up?"

"I was out Young's Park sitting in my homeboy's truck when I saw her running down Virginia Beach toward Monticello Avenue with her wrists tied up and duct tape covering her mouth. I asked her what was up and if she needed some help. She said yeah, so I untied her wrists and ripped off the fucking tape."

"What made you bring her here?"

"I told him I needed a burner."

Walt looked back at Fro. "You told her I had burners and you didn't even know her?"

"Nah, Walt, you know I don't carry it like that. I just told her that I could get her one, and when we pulled up to your crib, that's when she told me she knew you."

"Yeah, he's not lying. When we pulled onto Reservoir, I automatically knew he was coming to see you."

Walt asked me again how I got banged up. And he wanted to know who did it. I took a deep breath and told him everything I'd told Fro. I could tell Walt had trouble believing what I was saying. He looked back at Fro at least four times while I was talking.

When I was done speaking, Walt looked at Fro again and said, "I don't know why you did it, but you did the right thing by bringing her here to me."

Fro nodded.

"You know she's like a daughter to me, right?"

"She told me."

Walt started rubbing my back in a circular motion. "I used to mess with her mama back in the day. Unfortunately, it didn't last, so she was taken away from me after her mother moved out." He grabbed me and pulled me into his arms, embracing me like he didn't want to let me go.

"That's too bad," Fro said.

Walt asked Fro to step outside, so he could talk to him. After they walked out the back door, I dried the tears from my eyes and began to think about how I was going to take revenge on the motherfuckers who'd tortured me. I had so much anger and bitterness in my heart, I knew I could destroy anything. I didn't have a plan at all, but I decided I would figure that out as soon as I got my hands on a burner.

LOOKING OVER
YOUR SHOULDERS

Walt stayed outside with Fro for about five minutes, and when he came back into the house, Fro was nowhere in sight. Walt told me he'd sent him on his way.

"But I wanted him and his friend to take me to my rental car," I said.

"He already told me. Don't worry about it. I'm gonna take care of everything."

I stood. "Can I use your bathroom? I need to wash off this blood on my face and get myself together."

"Yeah, sure. It's right down that hallway to your right. My facecloths are in the hall closet right across from the bathroom. You can take a shower if you want."

After he pointed me in the direction of the bathroom, I didn't hesitate to get in there. Before I went inside the bathroom, I grabbed a towel and facecloth from the hall closet.

When Walt noticed I was getting ready to take a shower, he said, "If you want to change into something more comfortable, I can lend you a T-shirt and a pair of my shorts."

"Yeah, that's fine," I told him after I realized he wasn't

that much bigger than me. I wouldn't have a pair of panties to put on, but that didn't matter. I felt really dirty, and all I wanted to do was wash the icky feeling off me.

Once I was undressed, I turned on the shower and slid inside. The water was perfect. I turned my back against the stream, and the pressure of the water massaged my back muscles, relieving some of my tension. Although I tried to enjoy my shower, my mind kept flashing back to what I had gone through earlier that day. How stupid was I to fall for all that bullshit? I couldn't believe that I'd allowed myself to get caught up like that. I was from the streets, so I knew the tricks of the trade. I knew how to read certain niggas when they looked funny, but I guess, since I'd been away, I'd lost my touch.

Even though I had been violated and beat up, I still had some willpower left. I badly wanted revenge on Tony, my uncle, Dré, and Kasey. I could taste it. But I wasn't naïve. I knew I wouldn't be able to conquer that mission alone.

I probably stayed in the shower for about twenty minutes, which was enough time for me to collect my thoughts. When I stepped out of the bathroom, Walt was in his bedroom shuffling things around. It sounded like he was rearranging some large objects. I stood in the hallway with the towel wrapped around me and knocked on his bedroom door.

"I'll be out in a minute," he said.

"I just need you to hand me those clothes you said you had for me."

"I put 'em on the bed in the other bedroom."

"OK, thanks," I said and walked away.

I went into the other bedroom and got dressed. The T-shirt was a little too big, and so were the shorts, but I needed something to cover my body, so I made do. After I slipped back on my ballet flats, I balled up the clothes I had on earlier and placed them on the edge of the bed. If there was a garbage can somewhere nearby, I would've thrown them out. I didn't need anything around me that reminded me what I'd gone through today, especially since I knew that I wasn't ever going to wear those clothes again.

When I came out of the bedroom, Walt was sitting in the living room talking on his cell phone. As soon as I approached him, he cut his conversation short and ended the call. He tapped a spot beside him on the sofa and told me to sit there, so I did.

"I just got off the phone with a friend of mine, and he agreed to help me with your problem."

I didn't respond. I just looked at him really strangely. I immediately began to wonder what type of plan they had come up with. When dealing with men like Walt, who liked to provide as little information as possible, you had to follow blindly. He'd been like that for years, and I didn't think he was going to change now.

"Do you need some ice for your mouth?" he asked me after focusing on the cheek and mouth areas of my face.

"No, I'm fine."

"You sure? Because that looks really bad."

"Yeah, I'm sure." I laid my mouth in the palm of my right hand to cover it.

"You know, you look just like your mother."

I gave him a nonchalant expression and shrugged. I wasn't in the mood to be reminded about how much I resembled my mother. I had just been sexually assaulted and tortured, so my mind was somewhere else.

"You know, I still think about her," he said.

"I'm sure you do."

Walt placed his hand on my right knee. "If me and your mama were still together, you would've had a different life, and she'd probably still be alive today."

"There's a strong possibility that you could be right."

"Damn! If I could only turn back the hands of time."

"You can't, so don't even dwell on it."

I took a deep breath and exhaled.

"I can't believe your uncle did some shit like that to you," he said, again. "I know your mother is turning over in her fucking grave right now."

I looked back at Walt. "I know she is too."

"Well, he's got to be dealt with. I can't sit here and know what he did to you and not do anything to him."

"I want a piece of his ass too." I knew Walt saw the vengeance in my eyes. I literally wanted to get a gun from him and go on a shooting rampage.

"Do you think he's at home?" Walt asked me.

"I'm not sure. What time is it?"

Walt looked down at his wristwatch. "Ten thirty."

"I've never known him to be out this late, but a lot

about him has changed, so I can't call it."

"He's gonna be very shocked when he sees me coming for his ass." Walt smiled. "You know, he and I don't see eye to eye."

"Nah, I didn't know that."

"Yeah, him and your grandmother caused me and your mama to break up."

"Really? I never knew that."

"Yeah, they stayed in our business. And the day your mama moved out of my house, me and your uncle almost got into a fistfight."

"Are you serious?"

"Hell, yeah! He had just come home from the military, and he and your grandmother came to my house talking shit, telling your mama she didn't need to be with me, and that if she didn't leave with them, they were going to take you from her."

Shocked, I looked at Walt and said, "My grandmother threatened to take me away from my mama?"

"Yep, she sure did."

"Why? I mean, what was my mama doing so bad that my grandma would threaten to take me away from her like that?"

"They didn't like me, baby girl. They thought I was a bad influence because I was in the streets hustling, and they didn't want y'all around it."

"Well, if you look at it from their perspective, you'd probably feel the same way."

"Listen, baby girl, I'm not a petty-ass nigga. If the

shoe was on the other foot, I would've probably acted the same way. But the part I didn't like was when your uncle pulled a gun on me and stuck it in my face. I swear, if your mama hadn't defused the situation, I would have run in my house, grabbed my pistol, and blew his motherfucking head off his shoulders."

"Wow! It got that bad?"

"Hell, yeah! The police came and everything."

"Wait a minute. Where was I? Because I don't remember any of that happening."

"You were in school."

"You know what . . . I questioned my mama over a dozen times about why we were moving back to my grandmama's house, but all she did was brush me off. As time passed, I just stopped asking her, because she never gave me a straight answer. And when I started seeing you again after I got married, knowing what really happened back then between y'all wasn't a top priority anymore, so I left it alone."

"Well, I didn't want to leave it alone. I wanted to tear some shit up. I especially wanted to kill Lanier because of how he disrespected me. I have never allowed a man to stick a pistol to my head and then walk around and talk about it. That's a no-no in my world."

"My husband Ricky felt the exact same way. He used to always tell the flunkies who worked for him that if they ever pulled out a gun on somebody, they'd better use it, or they'd be the ones on the chopping block."

"Baby girl, that's the number one cardinal rule for the streets, so your uncle was one lucky motherfucker!"

"Well, you know what?"

"What?"

"His luck just ran out, because I'm getting ready to serve his ass to you on a silver platter."

Before Walt could respond to my comment, his cell phone rang. He looked at the caller ID screen then answered, "What's up, Griff?"

I couldn't hear what the caller was saying, but whatever it was, it was something Walt wanted to hear.

"OK, that's what I'm talking about, brother." Walt smiled. "Come on through. I'll be waiting for you." He then disconnected the call.

"You ready to take a ride?" he asked me.

"I guess so," I responded, not knowing what was about to transpire. I did know that Walt was about to create a lot of bloodshed, and this time it wasn't going to be my blood.

While we waited for Griff to arrive, Walt went into the kitchen and grabbed a beer from the refrigerator. "Want something to drink?"

"You got bottled water?"

"Yeah."

"I'll take one of those then."

Five seconds later Walt walked back into the living room with his beer in one hand and my bottled water in the other. He handed me the water and sat back down on the sofa next to me.

After he sipped and swallowed some of his beer, he looked at me and asked, "How long has it been?"

"What are you talking about?"

"Since I seen you."

I thought for a second. "It's been a few years now."

Walt fell silent and thought for a second.

"Yeah, you're right, because the last time we talked was when I gave you and Ricky those tickets to the Redskins game."

I nodded. "Yeah, you're right. Wow! That was at least two years ago."

He nodded too. "Yep." He took another sip of his beer.

After he swallowed the beer, he switched the subject on me. I knew it was coming. I just didn't know when. And what was even crazier about it was, I wasn't prepared for it. Walt was a very straightforward guy and held back no punches, which was why he would forever be respected.

"Tell me what went down with that federal case you and Ricky was involved in."

"What do you want to know?" I asked, trying to buy some time. I figured he'd heard a lot of different stories on the streets, a lot of which, I was sure, were blown out of proportion.

"Just tell me everything."

Knowing that he wanted me to tell him everything almost drove me to throw up all over his carpet. I didn't want him to label me a snitch. And I definitely didn't want him to throw me out of his house and renege on helping me with my problem. I needed him. He was the only person left in my life that I could trust. Too bad I hadn't thought about him before now. I guess when you stay out of touch with people for long periods of time, you tend to forget about them.

I had to give God the credit for this one. He knew I needed help, so He used a total stranger like Fro to bring me to Walt. Funny how life worked.

I took a deep breath and exhaled. I opened my mouth, but nothing came out. Walt gave me his full, undivided attention, and there was no other way around it. I had to come clean with him, so I did. Well, I almost did.

He blurted out, "Just tell me what they said about you on the streets wasn't true."

"What did you hear?" I thought turning the question back on him would take me off the hot seat and relieve some of the pressure for a moment.

But Walt didn't fall for my tactics. "You know I don't get into all of that," he said. "I never repeat shit I hear. That's why I go to the source. Now tell me what happened," he said, looking me straight in the eyes.

I instantly felt a lump form in my throat, and I felt sweat seeping through my pores from my armpits. I did my best to remain calm, because Walt was a pro when it came to sniffing out a liar. I didn't want that to happen with me, so I held my composure and pulled myself together.

"Well, what happened was, my cousin Nikki got caught transporting some product for Ricky, so when the narc busted her, they locked her up, refusing to give her bail because they knew the feds would pick up her case. So when the feds picked up the case, Nikki got scared. She freaked out and started telling everything she knew about Ricky's drug dealings, so she wouldn't have to do time. And when the indictments came through, everybody but me got arrested."

"Why is that?"

"Why is what?" I asked, knowing damn well what he meant. I tried to throw a stupid card out there to see if he'd bite.

"Why didn't you get arrested?"

"Because she told them I had nothing to do with his organization. She told them I didn't even know that she was transporting drugs for him. She said she went behind my back and did it."

"And the feds bought that story?"

"Evidently they did, because they didn't touch me. Now, they came by my shop and harassed me a few times to see if what Nikki was telling them was a lie, but other than that, they didn't fuck with me."

Walt stared deep into my eyes. I'd heard people say that you could tell when a person was lying by looking into their eyes, so I guessed that was what he was trying to do. I just acted normal and rode with it.

"When did you get out of the Witness Protection Program?"

Oh my God! Now where in the hell did that question come from? I'd never mentioned to anyone that I was in that program but my immediate family. But apparently word got into the streets. I hadn't spoken to Walt or seen him for two years, so I knew this was a trick question. It was a test to see if I snitched, even though I claimed that I hadn't. No one went into the Federal Witness Protection Program unless she was an informant who needed to be protected from the niggas she testified against. Or if she was an innocent bystander who witnessed something that could cost her her life, which wasn't my case. Those are the two options. That was it, cut and dry.

I looked at Walt like he was out of his damn mind. "I was never in the Witness Protection Program. I mean, don'tcha have to testify against someone and be afraid for your life to go into something like that?"

Walt looked deeper into my eyes. "That's what they say." He took another sip of his beer. "Then where did you disappear to?"

"What do you mean? I was home," I lied.

"You sure? I mean, you know you can tell me anything. I used to take care of your butt just like you were mine, so you know your secret is safe with me."

"So did my uncle, and look what he did to me," I said underneath my breath.

"You say something?"

"I just said I know I can trust you."

Walt poured the last of his beer into his mouth and set the bottle on the coffee table. He looked back at me without blinking. I was extremely uncomfortable, but I didn't let him know it.

"I read in the newspaper that Ricky got murdered by a couple dudes from a Spanish mob," Walt said. "Was that true?"

I sighed heavily. "That's what I was told."

"Why you think they did it? Did he owe them money?"

"Not to my knowledge. I don't think he owed anybody."

"Think he turned snitch?"

"Walt, I can't tell you what Ricky had going on. He pretty much kept me out of the loop with everything dealing with the streets. The only thing he couldn't keep from me was all those bitches he fucked around with."

Walt was about to comment, but a knock on the back door prevented him from doing so. "I'll be right back," he told me and stood. He headed toward the back door.

While he went to see who it was at the door, I let out a loud sigh. I felt like he'd had me in a fucking chokehold while questioning me, and that wasn't a good feeling.

Walt returned to the living room, accompanied by a young guy, who looked to be around twenty-five or twenty-six. Average height and clean-cut, he reminded me of the comedian Mike Epps. He looked at me with a serious expression. He was definitely here on business.

"Griff, this is my stepdaughter, Kira. She's the one I was telling you about."

Griff nodded. "What's up?"

"Hey."

Walt asked me, "You ready?"

"Yes." I didn't know why, but my heart started beating like crazy.

"Go ahead and follow Griff outside. I'll come out in just a minute." Walt headed down the hallway that led to his bedroom. He didn't have to tell me he was going in the back to retrieve his pistol, or whatever type of machinery he had stashed away. I knew him well enough to know that he wasn't going to leave his house without carrying something heavy-duty.

I was hesitant to follow Griff outside. Shit, I didn't know him from a can of paint. For all I know, he could've been there to kill me like my uncle and everyone else who had it in for me. But I took a chance. I figured if he got me after everything I'd been able to escape that night, then it really was my time to go.

There was a dark blue Caravan with tinted windows sitting outside. I saw a guy in the driver's seat waiting patiently. By the time we reached the van, Walt had come outside.

"When you get in, sit in the last row," Griff told me as he rolled back the door.

As I climbed into the back, I noticed that there were large sheets of heavy-duty plastic spread across the floor of the van and draped across the middle seat. Seeing this type of shit gave me the chills and made me want to step back out of the van and run as fast and as far as I could. I'd known cats who laid down large amounts of plastic in their vehicles because they didn't want blood to splatter all over the place after they'd butchered somebody. I was just hoping that it wasn't my blood they were after.

Walking across the plastic covering was pretty noisy, but I made the best of it.

Griff turned around in his seat to make sure I hadn't damaged the plastic in any way. The driver didn't look my way at all. He didn't turn around one time to see who I was or how I looked. That shit gave me the creeps, but, hey, what was I supposed to do? I couldn't get back out of the van and tell them I didn't need their help. They would've looked at me like I was fucking crazy, so I took a seat and said a quick prayer before we pulled off.

"Let's get the show on the road!" Walt said as he slid the van door closed and sat down in the row ahead of me.

DOING A DRIVE-BY

"Where we going first?" Griff asked from the front passenger seat.

"Let's ride out to Huntersville first," Walt said. "I want to see if these niggas are still at the spot where they had her."

Knowing we were on our way to the house where I had been held and tortured made me nervous. I thought about the possibility of falling back into the hands of my uncle or one of those retarded-ass niggas if Walt's plan went sour. I didn't like the thought at all, so I tried to block it out of my mind.

There I was in the back of a van about to witness a fucking bloodbath. If I wasn't angry and bitter, I would not have been able to take that ride with them. I was the type of chick that didn't like controversy. That was why so many niggas used to get over on me. I was used to sweeping shit under the rug, so I wouldn't have to deal with it.

But tonight I felt different. I was tired of being walked on. I needed to show motherfuckers I wasn't a woman that could be pushed down and abused. And I meant that from the bottom of my heart.

Walt didn't live that far from Huntersville. The drive from his house to the spot where I was couldn't be more than two miles, if that. During the course of the drive, while Walt made comments about their plan, I kept looking out the window, pretending I was uninterested.

"You got all the tools we gon' need?" Walt asked.

Without turning around, Griff said, "Yes."

I wanted to know what kind of tools they were talking about. Since Walt was the go-to man when it came to getting burners, they had to be talking about something other than guns.

While I racked my brain trying to figure out what they were talking about, Griff pulled out two loaded pistols, laid them across his lap, and began to do an overall inspection of them. I heard him eject the magazine, and then I heard him push it right back into the handle. Then he performed the same routine with the other pistol. I couldn't see what kind of semi-automatic weapons they were, but from the sound of them, I assumed they would do the job.

"Which street do we turn on?" the driver asked.

Walt turned around and looked at me. "Which street did you say it was?"

"The house is on B Avenue."

"Which side?" the driver asked.

Walt turned around and looked at me again. Before he could repeat the driver's question, I blurted out, "It's the third house on the left."

The driver slowed down at the corner of Church

Street and B Avenue and then made a right turn. My heart started beating uncontrollably as soon as we approached the house. To my surprise all the lights were out, and it looked deserted. My chances of seeing those animals getting paid back for all the shit they'd put me through began to look slimmer and slimmer by the minute.

"It doesn't look like anybody is there," I said.

The driver slowed down a little bit more.

"She's right," Griff said.

"What y'all want me to do?" the driver asked.

Walt told him, "Circle around the block one time."

"Whatcha wanna do that for?" Griff asked.

"I wanna see if any one of those niggas is walking around in the streets."

"Well, we might as well drive down every block, if you wanna see that."

"A'ight. Well, let's do that then," Walt said.

After getting the OK from Walt, the driver pressed down on the accelerator. He drove down every street in Huntersville. Every block and side street this place had, we were on it, but we had no luck finding the motherfuckers who'd assaulted me.

At the end of every street we drove through, Walt shook his head.

After the driver had driven down every street in Huntersville, he pulled over on the side of Goff Street and asked Walt where he wanted to go next.

Walt looked back at me. "You ready to pay that Tony guy a visit?"

I tried to reply, but I got a lump in my throat, so I had to give him a nod instead. But then I thought about it. I wanted to know if he planned to have me somewhere around so I could see the nigga's face when he was down on his knees, crying and begging for his life.

"I know we hadn't discussed it," I said, "but I was wondering how you planned to get Tony and my uncle. I mean, Tony may be easier than my uncle because he ain't gonna have his kids with him. I was with him when he dropped them off, so there's a good chance that he could be home alone, unless he got word that I escaped. And as far as my uncle is concerned, it would be crazy to go in his house when his wife is there, because if she saw one of y'all trying to take out her husband, she's going to scream or call the police. She's one crazy bitch! And I hate her fucking guts."

"Don't worry! We got all of that under control. Just sit back and relax, because all we're gonna do is ride by your uncle's house to see if he's there," Walt told me. "And if he is, we gon' go to Tony's place to snatch him up and use him to get your uncle to come out of his house."

"Oh, OK."

I sat back in the seat and watched as the driver took directions from Walt. My uncle lived in the plush part of Virginia Beach. His neighborhood was seventy-five percent Caucasian, ten percent black, and the other fifteen percent was a mixture of Hispanic and Asian. The houses in this community were priced at a half million dollars or more. For years, I wondered how he was able to afford his home on his salary as the general manager at Wal-Mart. When I finally found out that he stole a lot of high-end electronics from the warehouse and sold them on the streets, I almost fell out. I knew his self-righteous ass was into some type of illegal doings, and I didn't buy that bullshit act when he and his wife used to talk trash about Ricky. In my opinion, he acted like he was a bit jealous, because Ricky and I lived in a neighborhood similar to his, but we were so much younger than him.

The ride to my uncle's house took the driver approximately twenty minutes, but to me it seemed like forever.

"Make a left turn on the next street," I instructed the driver. I had a funny feeling that my uncle was two steps ahead of us, and was squatting somewhere in the bushes alongside his house, waiting patiently for us to drive by so he could do some damage.

"After you make the left, keep straight, and make another left at Evergreen Place," I said.

It seemed like the closer we came to Lanier's house, the more nervous and jittery I became. I was a fucking nervous wreck. I had never before ridden around in a van and pointed out niggas for another nigga to kill 'em. Hell, I was married to a fucking notorious gangster, and he didn't get involved with shit like this, so this was something new to me.

I pointed. "It's the fifth brick house on the right side."

"I don't see any cars in the driveway," Griff said.

"They probably got them inside the garage." Walt

turned around to face me. "Do they normally park their cars inside the garage?"

"Yeah, sometimes they do."

As we rode by, everyone in the van noticed that all the lights in the house were shut off, except for a light coming from a room on one side of the house.

Walt asked me, "Do you know what room that is?"

"Yeah, that's my uncle's study. That's where he keeps his computer, fax machine, and all the freaking books he collects."

"Well, it looks like he may be in the house after all," Walt said.

"You might be right," I said.

"All right, Jeff, let's get out of here," Walt said.

Jeff, the driver, very quickly jumped back on Highway 264 and headed toward Chesapeake. Walt asked me to give Jeff directions to Tony's house, so that was what I did.

Going back to Tony's apartment felt different this time around. I knew I wasn't going there for a friendly visit. All of the brotherly love I'd felt for him was gone. I couldn't care less about him anymore. It didn't matter to me that his kids were gonna be without a father. He had crossed the line, and I wanted to make sure he paid the consequences.

"Make a right turn at this next corner," I told Jeff.

It was pitch-dark outside, but the lamps from the tall light poles allowed us to navigate easily inside the small complex. The headlights from the van helped as well.

"I don't see my rental car," I blurted out. "He must've moved it." I stretched my neck forward to see.

"Where did you park it?" Walt asked.

I pointed toward a tall tree. "I parked it right there in that last parking space beside that tree." I looked inside my purse to see if my keys were still there. I shuffled everything around in my handbag, and then I shook it up and down to locate the keys to the car, but I came up empty-handed. "Ahh, shit! He took the keys out of my purse. And he got my hotel room key too. What the fuck am I gonna do now?"

Walt turned back around in the seat and grabbed my left hand. "Calm down, baby girl. Everything is gonna be all right."

"But you don't understand, Walt. This shit we're doing can come back and blow up in my face. I mean, I can get in a lot of fucking trouble if we get rid of Tony and then the police find my rental car later with his fingerprints all over it. You know I'm gonna be their number one suspect. And I'ma be honest with you, I'm not trying to be part of a murder investigation."

Walt released my hand and placed his finger against his mouth. "Shhh! I'm gonna handle everything."

I exhaled and sat back in the chair. By this time, Jeff had pulled the van to the curb.

"Do you see his car out here?" Griff asked.

I sat forward once again and strained my eyes so I could see better. I scanned the parking area and realized that Tony's car was nowhere to be found. I sat back in the seat and let out a big sigh. "Nah, it's not out there."

"What kind of car does he have?" Griff asked.

"He drives a sky-blue Toyota Camry."

Jeff turned off the ignition and then cut off the headlights. "I see a car coming in behind us. You think that could be him?"

Walt and I both turned around to look out the back window. "This car pulling up is smaller than a Camry." I watched the car slow down and then come to a complete stop.

"What they doing?" Walt asked.

"It's a lady, and she looks like she's trying to figure out where to park her car," I said, refocusing my eyes. "Oh shit! That looks like Shannon, Tony's girlfriend."

"Is she alone?" Griff asked.

"Yeah, she's by herself."

Walt grabbed both of his guns from the seat beside him. He stuck one in the waist of his jeans and screwed a silencer into the other one. I saw Griff handling his gun too. After he took off the safety, he screwed a silencer into the barrel of his pistol, and then he placed the gun in his right hand and waited for Walt to make the call.

"Wait until she gets out her car and walks past the van before you jump out on her," Walt instructed.

"What we gon' do? Drag her in her house?" Griff asked.

"Nah, we gon' drag her ass in this fucking van."

"What we gon' do if she screams?"

"If you put your pistol in her mouth, the bitch ain't gon' be able to scream."

Jeff looked back at Walt. "You got a point there."

"I still think she might try to scream," Griff said.

"Well, if she does, just hit her in the back of her fucking head. That'll shut her up real quick."

Walt was right. Getting hit in the back of the head with a blunt object would definitely shut up a person. I'd had my share of hits in the back of my head, and that shit ain't no joke. It wouldn't surprise me at all if I went to the doctor later on in life and found out that I had some type of brain damage.

After a couple minutes Shannon found a parking spot. When she stepped out of the car, she was having a conversation on her cell phone, the phone pressed against her right ear. I thought maybe that's why it had taken her so long to park in the first place. Whatever the caller was saying to her had to be funny, because she was smiling from ear to ear.

After she ended her call, she stuck her phone inside her handbag, reached inside her car, and grabbed her shopping bags. It looked as if she had just come from the supermarket. I could see a gallon of milk sticking out of one of the four bags bag she was struggling to carry.

"Here she comes," Walt announced.

Knowing what was about to go down, I got scared, although I couldn't explain why. I mean, I couldn't care less about this dumb-ass bitch. She wasn't related to me, and she was very rude to me earlier, so I really didn't care what happened to her.

As Shannon approached the right side of the van, Walt and Griff waited patiently for her to get close enough so they could apprehend her. I sat back and counted each step she made in my direction. When I got to twelve, Walt and Griff both opened their doors and jumped out of the van.

Totally caught off guard, Shannon screamed, dropped her grocery bags, and tried to make a run for it, but Griff stopped her in her tracks, grabbing her by the back of her neck and pointing his gun directly at the back of her head. "If you scream again, I'ma blow your fucking head off!"

Shannon buckled at the knees and almost collapsed, but Walt came up from behind and grabbed her by the arm. "A'ight, I gotcha,' he said, "so take a couple steps backward."

Cooperating like she was told, Shannon took the steps backward until she was close enough to the van to get inside. Walt grabbed her by both of her hands and turned her around to face the opening of the van. Her eyes immediately connected with mine. When she realized who I was, she acted like she'd seen a ghost or something. She must have been surprised to see me as one of her kidnappers.

I turned my head to look out the window as soon as I saw Walt pull out the gray electric tape to tie her wrists together. I waited for her to make a comment or say something to me, but she kept her mouth closed and allowed them to do whatever they wanted.

When Walt instructed her to get into the van, she did that with no problem, taking a seat in the chair in front of me. Griff picked up her bags of groceries from the ground and threw them in the back of the van where I was sitting. Then he and Walt hopped back into the van.

"Walt, you think anybody saw us?"

"Nah, I don't think so."

"I don't think so either," I said, "because as soon as she screamed, I looked around outside to see if anyone was looking."

Walt sat down beside Shannon and pointed his pistol directly into her face, and Griff turned around in his seat and pointed his gun at her too. I knew they weren't about to shoot her, but they sure acted like they were. Their faces showed no emotions, but you could tell that they meant business.

"Where is your boyfriend?" Walt asked her.

"I don't know. I haven't seen him since earlier when I left the house to go to work." She began sobbing.

"So you're telling me you haven't talked to him all day?" Walt asked.

"I talked to him twice during my breaks, but we didn't stay on the phone long."

"Did he tell you where he was?" Griff asked.

With tears falling from her eyes, Shannon looked to the front of the van and answered Griff's question. "No, he didn't say where he was, but he did say he had a run to make, and he would be home when I got here."

I heard the sincerity in her voice, so I knew she wasn't lying. I believed Walt knew she was telling the truth too, because he came at her with a different approach.

"Where is your cell phone?"

"In my purse."

Walt lowered the gun from her head as he reached into her purse to retrieve her cell phone. When he located it, he pulled it out and held it toward her. "What's his number?"

"Five, five, five, seven, eight, two, zero," she said between sniffles.

Walt entered the digits. Before he pressed the send button, he gave Shannon specific instructions to find out Tony's whereabouts, and then tell him to meet her at a remote location nearby because her car cut off. He also stressed to her that if she screamed or gave any indication that she was being held hostage, he would splatter her brains everywhere without thinking twice.

She understood everything he said and she knew he meant every word, because as soon as Tony answered his phone, she sat straight up and cleared her throat, and tried to act normal. Walt had Tony on speakerphone, so we could hear the entire conversation.

"Baby, where you at?" she asked. Her voice cracked a little bit, but she regained control.

"I'm taking care of some business. Why?"

"I'm calling you because my car cut off on me, so I need you to come get me."

"Whatcha mean, your car cut off on you? Are you out of gas?"

"No, I think it might be my alternator, or maybe I might need a jump."

"Where you at?" he asked, even though it seemed like

he was preoccupied with something else.

"I'm not too far from the house."

"Well, get out the car and walk to the house. I'll come get you later, so we can try to give it a jump."

Walt shook his head and then muted the phone so Tony wouldn't hear him. "No, tell him he needs to come get you now. Let him know that it's too late for you to be walking out here alone."

"Hello," Tony said after the brief silence.

Walt quickly took the phone off mute.

"I'm here," Shannon said.

"So whatcha gon' do?"

"Tony, it's too late for me to be walking out here in the dark like this. You need to come get me now," she yelled.

Tony sighed. "Yo, give me twenty minutes, and I'll be there."

"But you don't even know where I'm at."

"Oh shit! My bad! Where you at?"

Walt muted the phone again. "Tell 'im you on Providence Road in the same shopping center where Upscales is."

"Hello?"

Walt un-muted the phone again.

"Yeah, I'm here."

"What's wrong with your phone?" he asked, sounding agitated.

"Ain't nothing wrong with my phone."

"If ain't nothing wrong with it, then why does it keep going in and out?"

"I don't know."

"Well, you need to have that shit checked out. Now tell me where you at."

"I'm on Providence Road near Upscales."

"Where 'bout?"

"I'm at the end of the shopping center. You'll see my car."

"A'ight. I'll be there in a few."

"OK."

Walt took the phone from her ear and pressed down on the end button. "Griff, you gon' have to drive her car down to Providence Road."

"A'ight, give me her keys."

Walt looked at Shannon and asked her for her car keys.

"I stuck 'em in my purse."

When Walt had her keys in his hand, he handed them to Griff. "You got your gloves?" Walt asked him.

"Yeah, they in my pocket."

"Well, don't forget to put 'em on before you get into her car."

"I'm putting them on as we speak."

"Are y'all gonna kill me?" Shannon asked before Griff got out of the van.

I felt her pain, because I had been in the same situation a handful of times during my life. I knew how it felt, wanting to know if you were about to take your last breath.

Walt turned and looked at Griff, and then he looked back at Shannon. The next thing I know, he raised his gun and pointed it directly at her face.

She started crying instantly. "Please don't kill me! I'll do anything you ask."

I closed my eyes and put my face in my hands. I knew Walt was about to take her out, because of the blank expression on his face.

"Please! Please!" she kept saying.

Then, all of a sudden, I heard a loud *Thump!*

I wanted to remove my hands from my face, but I wasn't sure if he'd shot her in the head or what. I wasn't prepared to see her brains splattered all over the place.

"You can take your hands away from your face," Walt said to me.

"Nah, I'm all right."

Griff laughed. "She doesn't want to see all that blood."

"Well, she better get used to it, because tonight is going to be a long night."

Right after Walt made his comment, I heard him move around in the van, and then I heard him rattle the plastic. I didn't have to see what he was doing to know he was moving Shannon's body so he could wrap her in the plastic. He made enough grunting noises to let me know that he was struggling to accomplish his mission. I heard Griff climb back from the front seat to help him.

"Grab that end of the plastic while I lay her this way," Walt said.

"Why don't you just roll her this way, while I fold the plastic that way?"

"A'ight."

The rattling of the plastic lasted for another ninety seconds, and then it stopped. I decided to move my hands. I looked straight down to the floor of the van and noticed that Shannon was indeed dead and wrapped tightly in the industrial-strength plastic. Thank God, I couldn't see any of her blood, because I don't think I would have been able to handle it. I'd seen my cousin Nikki as she lay dying in a puddle of her own blood, which had messed me up pretty badly already.

"Where you wanna dump her body?" Griff asked.

"We can dump her in that wooded area on South Military Highway behind that salon called Star Struck," Walt suggested.

"Oh, yeah, that's a good spot. Ain't nobody gonna find her for at least a couple months," Griff said as he crawled back into the front seat. "I'm gon' go ahead and get in her car before somebody drives up and sees me."

"Yeah, go ahead and take her car down there to Providence Road, and me and Jeff will meet you there in about ten minutes."

"You better make it sooner than that. I don't want her nigga rolling up on me and I'm by myself."

"Nigga, don't let me find out you scared!" Jeff joked.

Walt laughed. "Come on, don't talk like that. You know you'd be able to handle things without us."

"I know I can too, but I ain't trying to take the chances of that nigga rolling up on me while he got somebody with him."

"He's right," I chimed in. "Tony sounded like he was

with someone, so there's a big possibility that he may come with that person."

"You better listen to her, Walt," Griff said.

Walt thought for a second and then said, "All right, just follow me and Jeff to that spot, so we can get rid of this body, and then we'll head down to Providence together."

"A'ight." Griff got out of the van and ran over to Shannon's car.

Jeff sped out of the parking lot, and Griff followed. We were only three miles from the wooded area, so it only took us about five minutes to get there.

As soon as we arrived at the wooded area, Griff parked Shannon's car on the opposite side of the street, and then he raced across the street to where Jeff had parked the van. Walt opened the side door of the van, while Griff and Jeff stood outside to help him dispose of the body. They all wore dark clothing, so it was hard to see them in the dark.

After they removed Shannon's body from the van, they started walking into the thick thicket of trees that sat about two hundred feet from the highway. It soon became difficult for me to see them.

A couple cars rode by while they were away from the van, and my heart jumped all over the place while my stomach did some flips. I knew I was in the wrong, but I still prayed to God that a police car wouldn't ride by and get suspicious because of the van being parked at such a remote location.

Curiosity was killing the hell out of me. I wanted to know where they left her body. It wasn't like I wanted to go back and locate her body or anything, but I wanted to be included. I took the ride, so why couldn't I know what went on out there? I knew how to keep secrets.

Immediately after they returned, Walt and Jeff jumped back into the van, and Griff hopped back into Shannon's car. Jeff whipped the van around and had us back on the main highway in less than four seconds flat. I looked out the back window and saw that Griff had turned around Shannon's car to follow us.

Our destination on Providence Road was about a six-minute drive. When we got there Walt asked me, "What color is his car again?"

"It's sky-blue. Why?"

"Do you see it?"

I looked around the entire parking lot of the nightclub, Upscales, and Tony's Camry was nowhere in sight. "Nope, I don't see it."

Walt exhaled. "Good. We beat 'im here." He got on his cellular phone and called Griff to give him further instructions. He told Griff to park Shannon's car, with the tail facing the street, and to lift up the hood. That way, when Tony drove up, he'd only see the car from behind.

Griff did exactly what Walt instructed him to do, and then we all sat back and waited patiently for Tony's arrival.

The twenty minutes he said it would take him to arrive at the location seemed like they took forever. I looked at the clock on the stereo system in the front of the van at least ten times, and every time I looked at it, the time would only show it to be a minute later than the previous time I looked.

Everyone sat in the van and said nothing. It was so quiet, I could hear Jeff when he inhaled and exhaled. And every time a car drove up, we all turned around to see if it was Tony, but it never was.

While we all sat quietly in the van, Walt got the urge to call Griff on his cell phone. When Griff answered, Walt put the call on speakerphone and said, "I think you need to get out of the car and act like you're doing something underneath the hood."

"But he might see me," Griff said.

"From the way you got her car parked, you can't see who's underneath the hood."

"Yeah," Jeff said, "tell 'im homeboy ain't gon' be able to see him."

"Jeff just said you a'ight, nigga, so stop whining." Walt laughed.

"I think you should come out here with me, just in case that nigga got a burner on him."

"Yeah, he's right, Walt. Tony might have a gun," I said.

Walt thought for a second and then said, "I'ma send Jeff out there just in case shit gets ugly."

"A'ight."

Walt hung up.

"How you want me to be positioned?" Jeff asked.

"Both of y'all need to lean over like y'all are working on something underneath the hood, so when homeboy show up, y'all can catch him off guard and ambush him."

"A'ight, I can do that. But why don't we pull this van up beside it and act like we giving that car a jump?

Remember, homegirl told that nigga that her car needed a jump."

Walt nodded. "Yeah, that's a good idea. Let's do that."

Jeff pressed down on the accelerator and drove the van right up to Shannon's car, but before he could get out of the driver's seat, a car with bright headlights rolled up behind us.

I immediately turned around. My heart skipped a beat when I realized it was Tony driving toward us. "It's him."

Walt and Jeff both tried to use their side mirrors to see the car behind us.

"Is he alone?" Walt asked.

"Yes, he's alone," I said quickly.

"All right, Jeff, we gon' have to do this real easy," Walt said slowly as he continued to look in his side mirror.

"Whatcha want me to do?" Jeff asked.

"Has he gotten out of the car yet?" Walt asked, sounding worried.

"Nah, not yet," I told him.

"What is he doing?"

"I can't see because he still got on his headlights," I replied.

After a minute I said, "Wait, I see him moving in the front seat like he's looking for something." I turned my head and looked through the front windshield to see what Griff was doing, but I couldn't see him at all. I figured he was staying out of sight, so he wouldn't blow his cover.

Finally Tony got out of the car. I looked directly at his

hands to see if he was carrying a weapon of some kind, but he wasn't. I alerted Walt to what I saw. Both Jeff and Walt sat in the front seat while Tony approached us.

We were parked directly beside Shannon's car, and there wasn't much room to walk between the car and the van, so Tony walked on the left side of Shannon's car.

Jeff looked at Walt. "You think we should get out now?"

"Yeah, come on."

By the time Jeff and Walt opened their door, Tony had gotten around to the front of Shannon's car.

"Who are you? And where is Shannon?" Tony asked.

I couldn't see what was going on because Griff had the hood open, but I could hear them. When Jeff and Walt got out of the van, I saw Jeff run around the left side of Shannon's car while Walt came around at another angle. They both had their guns drawn, so they were ready for whatever came next.

Tony yelled, "What the fuck!"

Then I heard some struggling. My first reaction was to jump out and see what was going on, but I decided against that, because I didn't want to be hit by a random bullet. My heart was pumping like crazy, and my curiosity was getting the best of me.

A minute later I saw Tony walking toward the van, Walt and Jeff following behind him. When Walt opened the van door for Tony to get inside, and Tony saw me sitting in the back of the van, he looked like he was seeing a ghost. When niggas got caught in the wrong, they always looked like they'd seen a ghost.

I shook my head at that clown. "You weren't expecting

to see me, huh?"

Walt hit Tony in the back of the head with the butt of his pistol, and Tony went out like a light. He stuffed his gun inside the waist of his jeans and asked Jeff to help him put Tony inside the van.

"Griff, can you straighten out the plastic on the floor?" Walt asked.

Griff jumped inside the van and turned around the plastic.

"Hurry, before somebody comes up," Walt said.

We were in the parking lot of a popular nightclub, and even though it wasn't open, we were near a very busy street, so someone was bound to drive by any second. With that in mind, I turned around in my seat and stared out the back window to make sure no one was coming.

After Griff straightened the plastic on the floor of the van, he climbed to the front of the van and waited for Jeff and Walt to lay Tony on top of it. Then Walt tied together Tony's wrists and legs.

"Whatcha want to do with the car?" Griff asked.

"Just close the hood, lock the door, and leave it there," Walt said. "A tow truck will snatch it up after midnight, since the club ain't open."

Once Griff was done following Walt's instructions, he got back in the van.

"Where we going now?" Jeff asked.

"Let's head back to Huntersville so this nigga can show us where those other motherfuckers are," Walt said.

"A'ight."

THE NEXT STEP

I sat in the backseat of the van in total amazement. I couldn't believe I had gotten myself caught up in kidnapping and murder. This wasn't how I wanted to live my life. All I ever wanted was a simple life. I never asked for much, and I'd never had it in me to hurt people. That wasn't how I was raised. So why was I always getting the fucked-up end of the stick? The only reason I came back to Virginia was to attend my cousin's funeral and pay my respects, but somehow I'd gotten more than I bargained for. Once my uncle had me kidnapped, I couldn't let it go and just return back to Anguilla. I had to have my revenge.

I looked at Tony while he lay on the floor and wondered what Walt had in store for him. Deep down in my heart I wanted that bastard to pay for all the pain and agony I'd gone through because of him, and it didn't matter what method Walt used to terminate him. All that I asked was that I got a chance to ask him one question before he took his last breath.

Ten minutes into the drive back to Norfolk, Tony started regaining consciousness. Walt sat in the seat above where he lay on the floor. He moved his head from side to side, and then he wiggled his body a little, once he realized he'd been tied up. It was hard to get a good look at him while the interior light was off in the van.

"Owww! Shit! My damn head hurts like a motherfucker!"

Walt leaned forward. He looked like he was about to get down on his knees, but he didn't. He was close enough to Tony's face so Tony could see who he was. "You lucky we ain't killed you."

I was sure Tony was still seeing red and blue stars, because he kept blinking his eyes while he tried to focus in on Walt.

"Come on, man," Tony said. "I got three grand in my front right pocket. I'll give it to you if you let me go."

Walt and Griff both burst into laughter.

"That was a nice offer, homeboy, but we already confiscated that." Walt waved the roll of fifty-dollar bills in his face.

"A'ight, man. Well, can you let me go, please?"

"Not until you tell me where we can find the motherfuckers who tortured Kira," Walt said.

"If I tell you where they at, you promise you'll let me go?"

Walt turned around and winked his eye at me, and then he turned back around toward Tony. "You got my word, so start talking."

Tony lifted his head from the floor as far as he could, so he could look directly at Walt. "Who you trying to find first?"

"It doesn't matter, homeboy, just as long as you help

us locate every last one of them."

"A'ight, well, Dré is probably at his crib, and Breon is at the crib too."

"I wanna know where Kasey is at?" My mouth was dry, but it felt like I could taste revenge.

Tony's eyes focused over Walt's shoulders and landed directly on me. "I don't know where Kasey lives, but I know where she hangs out at."

I tapped Walt on his shoulder. "Let's get her first."

Walt smiled at me. "I gotcha covered, baby girl."

While Jeff followed the directions from Tony, I sat back and wondered how I would react when I got my chance with that Kasey bitch. A whole lot of torturing methods crossed my mind, but I knew I didn't have the stomach to go through with them. I figured I'd be satisfied to just bring her to tears.

When we arrived back in Huntersville, Walt and Jeff dragged Tony from the floor and sat him up on the seat in front of me. They did this, so he could guide them along the streets of Huntersville. He instructed them to drive down Johnson Road first.

"Drive slowly," Tony said, "'cause Kasey be hanging outside in front of her girl's crib, which is that brick duplex right there on the left."

Everyone in the van, including me, sat straight up to see if we saw Kasey standing outside. There were a couple of people standing at the curb, but they were all men. Jeff kept driving.

"She might be in the house," I said.

"Yeah, she might be inside the house," Tony repeated.

"It's too risky," Walt responded. "We can't take the chance of fucking with her while there's a crowd outside. We got too many witnesses."

"Yeah, he's right," Jeff said. "We got too many bodies hanging around. Let's go at this thing another way."

"Wait. There she goes," I blurted out when I saw her coming outside from the downstairs apartment.

Walt and Tony both turned to look out the side window as Jeff stepped on the brakes.

"Where she at?" Walt asked me.

"She's right there walking up to that guy on the bike," I said.

Kasey had changed clothes from earlier. Now she was wearing a green-and-yellow Oakland A's jacket with a pair of dark jeans and a dark-colored ball cap turned backward. If I hadn't seen her before, I would've sworn she was one of the boys hanging out on the block.

Jeff pulled the van over to the right side of the street. He didn't bother shutting off the ignition or the headlights, so I assumed we stuck out like a sore thumb.

Walt must've figured out the same thing, because he made mention of it. "Kill the headlights."

"Nah, we need to go around the corner and come back," Griff suggested.

"No, we can't take that chance," I said. "She might be gone by the time we circle the block."

Griff turned around and looked at Walt. "Wanna get out right here while Jeff circles the block?"

Walt looked at Griff, and then he looked at me. "If I give you a burner, do you think you'd be able to hold this motherfucker until we get back in the van?"

I thought for a second, and then I looked at Tony. His wrists and ankles were tied up, so there was no way in hell he could get away, even if I didn't have a gun pointed directly at him. "Whatcha think he's going to do while he's tied up like this?" I asked.

"He ain't gon' be able to do shit! I just thought it would be proper for you to hold your own shit, just in case," Walt said.

"Well, in that case," I said, and then I extended my hand toward him. He handed me a Ruger revolver. The motherfucker was heavy, but I managed to hold it without looking like I was inexperienced.

Right after Walt and Griff hopped out of the van, Jeff pulled off very slowly. I watched Walt and Griff as they walked away from the van, but I also used my peripheral vision to watch Tony. I wanted to be fully aware of my surroundings, just in case he tried to do some funny shit.

Two minutes into the drive, Tony got up the courage to open his mouth. It didn't matter to him that Jeff was in the van with us, because he knew that his life was on the line. I was utterly disgusted that he even had to breathe the same air I was breathing, but I left well enough alone, and allowed him to get his few seconds of fame.

"Kira, I know I was fucked-up for setting you up earlier. And I know I can't turn the clock back either, but if you give me a chance to redeem myself, I will."

I gritted my teeth before I uttered one word to this asshole. He wanted to redeem himself after he'd put my ass on the chopping block. He had no love for my ass earlier when he traded me off to four goons for some small cash. I had every right to put a bullet in his head right then, but I didn't. I couldn't wait to give him the same treatment I'd suffered.

I sucked my teeth. "Tony, spare me all the bullshit! You know damn well you don't give a fuck about me. You cared nothing about me when Rhonda and I were friends, and you couldn't care less about me now, so cut it out."

"No, Kira, you got it all wrong. I didn't want to set you up for real, but I was broke and I was about to get put out of my apartment. Your uncle came to me with the plan to snatch you up and put you in an abandoned house so he could get you to tell him the real story behind his daughter's murder. He called me right before he left to go to Houston to identify Nikki's body. And you wanna know something else? I didn't tell him yes until after he called me while he was there and told me that he had seen you."

"You think that makes it better?" I snapped. "You handed me over to some motherfuckers that wanted to kill me! And if I didn't escape, I would probably be dead now, so don't feed me that bullshit!"

"Kira, I swear I wanted to turn back around and help you after I saw Kasey knock you out. That whole shit kept playing in my mind the whole time after I walked out of that house."

"Yeah, what the fuck ever! Tell me anything. Because if it was bothering you that much, you would've come back for me."

"Yo, Kira, I swear if I could have, I would have. Breon and Dré weren't gonna let me walk back up in there and get you after I made the trade-off. They would've probably tried to kill me if I stepped back in there talking about I was taking you back out of there."

"Look, Tony, leave it alone. What's done is done. You already fucked up with me, so I ain't got nothing else to say."

Tony frowned. He looked like his whole world had just fallen apart around him. "You gon' let them kill me?" he asked.

I hesitated before I answered. I badly wanted to tell him that his ass was as good as gone as soon as he got my uncle on the phone and convinced him to meet us somewhere. But I didn't feel like it was my place to tell him what his fate would be. Walt was in charge of this mission, so he should be the one to tell him. And, besides, I wasn't in a position to pull the blinders off Tony anyway. As long as he believed that we weren't going to harm one hair on his head if he helped us, then he'd be a willing participant in helping us find Dré, Breon, and Uncle Lanier.

"Look, Tony, all you need to worry about is helping us find everybody, and you gon' be a'ight."

I had always been good at lying. So when Tony asked me if his life would be spared, it took little effort for me to tell him what he wanted to hear.

From the time I'd started dating my late husband, up until the time we got married, I was taught how to lie. He didn't know it, but he embedded that in me. He lied to me on so many occasions, the shit started rubbing off on me. And the way things looked, I was only gonna get better and better at it.

By the time Jeff rode around the block and made it back to the same spot where Griff and Walt had gotten out of van, the streets looked empty. There was no one in sight. Griff and Walt were nowhere to be found.

"What the fuck just happened?" I asked, directing my question to Jeff.

"Shit! That's a good question. But I don't know what to tell you." He continued to drive the van slowly.

"You think they got in a shootout?"

"If they did, we would've heard the shots being fired when we were riding down the next street over."

"Well, something happened. And I don't like this feeling I'm getting in my stomach," I said.

"I'm getting a weird feeling too," Jeff said. "But I don't know what the fuck to do."

"Well, whatever you do, don't stop." I looked out the window on either side of the van.

Jeff kept his foot on the accelerator the entire time, and before we knew it, we were off Johnson Street and right back on the next street we had just driven down. When we arrived at the corner to make the turn to drive back down Johnson Street again, he came to a complete stop at the stop sign.

"You're not gonna go back down there, are you?"

"I wasn't trying to, but I don't want to leave Walt and Griff hanging."

"Call one of their cell phones."

"I ain't got Walt's number, but I got Griff's."

"Well, call 'im then."

Jeff sat there at the stop sign and pulled out his cell phone.

I instantly became nervous. "You gon' stay right here at this stop sign and try to call him?"

"Yeah. Why?"

"I think you should move on and keep driving. If you sit at the stop sign, you gon' bring attention to yourself. Remember, we are the only ones out here."

"She's right," Tony said.

Jeff looked through the rearview mirror at Tony. "Nigga, shut the fuck up! Ain't nobody talking to you."

"Damn, champ. I was only trying to help,"

"Nigga, I ain't cha champ!" Jeff roared. "And so you know, I got this shit over here covered, so take your mind off me and worry about yourself."

"Yeah, a'ight."

I chuckled to myself after I heard Jeff break down Tony's dumb ass. The shit was funny as hell. And after I got my laugh on, I turned my attention back to Jeff. But before I could open my mouth to say something, Jeff had Griff on the phone.

"Nigga, where y'all at?" Jeff asked.

I couldn't hear Griff's response, but I knew he

couldn't be that far away, because as soon as Jeff pulled off from the stop sign, he drove to the next block, which was Washington Street, and made a right.

After he disconnected the call, I asked, "Where they at?"

"Griff said they were walking up Washington Street toward Church Street."

"Did they get Kasey?"

"He didn't say."

A few seconds later, Jeff pulled alongside the curb of Washington Street where Walt and Griff were waiting. They both jumped back into the van.

"Did you get her?" I asked.

Walt sat on the seat beside Tony. He acted like he was out of breath, but he managed to respond. "Nah, we didn't get her."

"What happened? And where did everybody go? It looked like a ghost town when we drove back by the spot we dropped y'all off at."

"As soon as Griff and I got out of the van, the narc drove right onto the block and everybody scattered like roaches. So me and Griff started running and cut through this old lady's backyard."

"Y'all didn't have time to snatch up Kasey?" I asked.

"Nah, 'cause when the narcs drove up, they came hard. One of the narcs drove an undercover car onto the sidewalk where them niggas was standing, while the other narc car drove up in the parking lot of that brick duplex. They didn't look my and Griff's ways at all. They were more focused on that duplex and them niggas that was standing outside."

"You think they ran up on Kasey?" I asked.

"Yeah, they did run up on her. I saw one of them big ass white boys slam her on the hood of his car and put handcuffs on her."

"So what we gon' do now?" I asked.

"There ain't shit we can do," Walt said. "She's gone downtown. And, besides, it's hot out Huntersville right now. Our best bet is to get the fuck out of here before one of them narcs tries to pull us over and arrest us for having all these motherfucking pistols."

"So you ready to bounce?" Jeff asked.

"Yeah, let's get the hell out of here," Walt answered.

I was becoming depressed. I really wanted Kasey's head, wanted to see her beg for her life. "So what's gonna happen now?"

Walt said, "We gotta move on to the next nigga's spot, since we can't get to that chick."

Out of everyone on my list, I wanted Kasey in the worst kind of way. It was burning me up inside that she'd gotten away like that. She was one lucky bitch.

BACK TO SQUARE ONE

The moment we exited Huntersville, Walt instructed Tony to show us where Dré lived. Turned out, Dré lived in Barraud Park, which was only a few blocks away from Huntersville. It only took us a couple of minutes to get there.

"What part of Barraud Park he live in?" Jeff asked.

Tony sat up in his seat. "Him and his girl live in the houses right by the play park, but they live on the left side of the street."

Jeff followed Tony's instructions, and when we drove onto the street where Dré lived, Tony pointed out the house. "You see that small yellow house with the light on in the living room?"

"Yeah," Jeff said. "Is that the house?"

"Yeah, that's it."

Griff turned around and looked at Walt. "What's the plan, Walt?"

"We gon' get Tony to call this nigga out the house, and then we gon' blast his ass."

Tony looked nervous as hell when he heard Walt's plan. He held his composure, though, and acted like he was willing to do anything to keep his ass out the hot seat.

"Come on, let's do it," he said.

Walt turned around and looked at me. I shrugged my shoulders and gave him a half-smile. Everybody in the van could tell that Tony was doing a little ass-kissing, trying to stay on Walt's good side for as long as he possibly could. And guess what, if the shoe was on my foot, I would have been doing the exact same thing.

After Walt coached Tony on what to say he dialed the number Tony gave him, placed the phone under Tony's mouth while it was on speakerphone, and waited for Dré to answer.

"Yo, what's good?" Dré asked as soon as he answered his line.

"Hey, yo, man, I know where Kira is," Tony said.

"Nigga, you bullshitting me?"

"Nah, I just saw her."

"Where?"

"I saw her go into the lobby of her hotel."

"Did you call Lanier and tell 'im?"

"Nah, not yet."

"Nigga, you better call him. You know he's out beating down the bricks to find her."

"I was gon' call him, but I wanted to call you first to see if you wanted to get with me so we could both go to him and try to get a finder's fee, since we the ones who saw her first."

"That nigga ain't gon' come off on no more money. He's already in the hole for five grand with me and Breon, so I say, let him deal with that shit on his own."

"Come on, Dré, do you know how valuable this chick is? I know for a fact that Lanier would come off some more dough to get his hands on her. Remember, he wants to get to her before she goes to the police."

"I understand all of that, but what if she done already went to 'em? We're fucked."

"Dré, man, I don't think she went to the cops, especially after the way I saw her walk up into that hotel. She looked like she was in a rush, to me."

"So what's your plan?" Dré asked.

"Well, I think we should get her ass and take her to Lanier."

"Now how the fuck you think we gon' pull that off when she's in a public place? I mean, it ain't like she's going to come running to us."

"Yo, Dré, man, I know whatcha saying, and I know it's gon' be really hard, but we can come off and make Lanier pay us top dollar for her if we play our cards right. So I say let's put our heads together and make this shit happen."

Dré fell silent for a minute.

We all sat there and waited for him to respond to Tony's offer. It was so quiet, you could hear a pin drop. All of us were too afraid to breathe hard for fear that Dré would hear us.

Finally he sighed. "Look, Tony, I don't know about this one," he said. "Fucking with her while she's at her hotel is a little too risky for me. And, besides, my girl just got home from work, so if I tried to leave the crib right now, she'd go the fuck off."

Tony saw how he was grasping for straws to get Dré to come outside, so he turned on his persuasiveness a little more. "Yo, Dré, man, I'll tell you what. Lend me your piece and I'll go get her my damn self."

"I thought you had one."

"I did. But I had to get rid of it because I found out it was dirty."

Dré sighed once again. "A'ight. I'ma let you use it this time. But you gotta be careful and bring back my shit."

"A'ight, nigga, I gotcha."

"Call me when you get outside."

"I'm about to pull up now," Tony told him. "I'm in a dark-colored minivan."

"Where your whip at?"

"I had to switch it up, just in case that bitch got the police looking out for my car."

"Oh, yeah, you're right."

"Nigga, I told you, you won't be dealing with no corny-ass navy boy."

Dré chuckled. "You're a funny cat."

"Call it what you like, but I got plenty of sense."

"Yeah, yeah, yeah. I'll be outside in a minute." Dré then hung up.

I looked at Tony when Walt took the phone from his ear. If I didn't know better, I would've thought he shit on himself, because he looked nervous as hell.

Walt wasn't paying any attention to Tony after he had served his purpose in luring Dré outside. I watched him and Griff load up their arsenal, making sure the safeties were off. Then they sat back, patiently waiting for Dré to approach the van.

I was nervous, and my stomach was doing one flip after the next. I was about to witness yet another murder.

"Somebody's opening the front door," Griff announced.

I sat back in the seat and peered through the curtains of the minivan. When Dré made himself visible by stepping onto his porch, my heart sank to the pit of my stomach. I knew right then and there that things were getting ready to get really ugly.

I looked at Tony, who had laid himself back in the seat. It appeared that he wanted to hide himself, but he was sitting in a seat that wasn't adjustable, and Walt seemed a little uneasy himself.

As Dré walked down the stairs of the front porch and made his way over to the van, I could sense he was becoming a little leery. His facial expression started changing as he got closer to the van. He slowed down, trying to see who was sitting in the front seat. Then he stopped in his tracks. He stood about four feet away from the van and yelled out, "Yo, Tee."

Walt looked at Tony and nudged him in the side with the barrel of his gun. "Answer him."

"Yo, nigga, what's up?" Tony asked, sounding forced.

Dré said, "Come outside the van."

I looked at Walt and Griff, and both of them seemed like they were ready to go to war.

"Whatcha want me to do?" Tony asked. "You heard

him tell me to get out of the van."

Griff looked back at Walt, and in a low whisper, he said, "We gon' have to blast him right where he is."

Walt nodded. Without saying one more word, he grabbed the door handle and pulled back on it to slide the door open. As soon as the door opened wide enough for Walt to get a full view of Dré, he pulled back on the trigger of his pistol. I didn't hear the shot being fired because Walt had attached the silencer, but I saw the shells from the bullets pop out of the top of the chamber.

As Walt got closer to emptying his magazine, Griff opened his door and began to release the bullets from his burner as well.

Tony immediately dove to the floor of the van. Dré got a chance to point and aim his pistol at Walt, but he was unable to pull back on the trigger before bullets riddled his body. To see his body grow weaker and weaker as each bullet entered it gave me a sense of satisfaction. He deserved every last one of those bullets Walt and Griff emptied out on him.

Once Dré hit the ground, and it was clear he was dead, Walt and Griff both closed their doors, and Jeff sped off like lightning.

"Walt, I see you weren't playing," Griff said.

"Hell nah! You saw how that nigga was acting. He knew some funny shit was going on, and that's why he stopped in his tracks and started calling Tony's name."

Griff chuckled. "You see I wasn't letting off his ass either."

"Yeah. I noticed how you pulled your burner out and came in for the kill," Walt said.

"Shit, man, I only did that because he threw up his burner and tried to let one off on you."

Walt reached forward and patted Griff on his shoulder. "You did good, man. You did real good."

"Anything for you, man."

As Jeff sped out of Barraud Park, Tony tried to ease his way back into the seat, but Walt stopped that move, pressing his feet against Tony's leg and telling him to keep his ass where he was.

I almost burst into laughter, but I kept my mouth closed. I wanted to remain serious, especially around Tony. I couldn't let that motherfucker see me grinning like everything was all peaches and cream. I wanted him to get the impression I was an evil bitch; that vengeance was mine.

"Who we getting ready to get now?' Griff asked Walt.

Walt turned around and looked at me. "Who's next, baby girl?"

I wanted to tell Walt that Breon would be next, but it was he who made it possible for me to get away when he tried to take down my uncle. I knew he really didn't want to participate when Dré helped Kasey sexually assault me. After replaying everything in my mind, I decided that I wanted to leave Breon alone and concentrate on Tony and Uncle Lanier.

"I'm ready to close the chapter on my uncle," I said.

Walt pointed to Tony. "What about this piece of shit right here?"

"We still need him as bait to get my uncle out of the house," I said.

Tony lifted his head from the floor, with the most pitiful expression on his face. "Please don't kill me, y'all. I got two kids that need me. Tell 'em, Kira. My shorties just lost their mother, so they gon' be lost without me."

One part of me felt really sorry for him, but the other wanted to spit right in his fucking face. Always out for himself, he wasn't shit, for real. And today I was going to be just like him—hard-core with no cares in the world. I ignored him and looked out the left side window. Walt kicked him in his side and told him to shut the fuck up, and that was what he did.

Ten minutes into the drive to Uncle Lanier's house, Walt instructed Tony to get up from the floor. Tony sat back up, but instead of being allowed to sit on the seat beside him, Walt made him stay on the floor. He took Tony's phone from his pants pocket and asked me for my uncle's cell phone number and then once again he prepped Tony on what to say. He also gave Tony a firm threat that if he disobeyed him in any way that he wouldn't hesitate to pump two bullets into the back of his head.

When my uncle answered, Walt pressed the speakerphone under Tony's chin. Tony tried to speak, but nothing came out. Walt nudged him in his side again. "Say something," he whispered, so my uncle wouldn't hear his voice.

My uncle said hello three times before Tony finally answered him.

"Oh, um, Lanier, this is Tony." He cleared his throat.

"What the fuck is wrong with you?" Lanier asked.

"Nothing."

"Well, when I was saying hello, why the fuck didn't you answer me?"

"Because I didn't hear you."

"Something must be wrong with your phone, because I said hello loud and clear."

"Yeah, you might be right, because my girl said the same thing about my phone earlier. But the reason why I called you is because I know you're looking for your niece, and I just saw her walk into the lobby of her hotel."

"How long ago was that?"

"About ten minutes ago."

"Was she with anybody?"

"Nah, she was by herself, and she looked like she was in a rush too."

"You think she's about to check out?"

"I'm not sure. That's a hard one to call."

"Where you at now?"

Walt muted Tony's phone and instructed him to tell my uncle that he was sitting outside in the parking lot of the hotel, and Tony did as Walt told him.

My uncle paused for a moment, and then he said, "You think she called the police?"

"I'm not sure, but if she did, they would've been here by now."

Lanier hesitated for several seconds before saying,

"It's been over two hours since she got away, so she could've gone to the police right after she ran off."

"I don't think she went to the police, because she pulled up in a cab. And I'm thinking, if she did get a chance to go to them, they would've had an officer escort her back to the hotel."

"Yeah, you're probably right. Stay right there, and I'll be there in about twenty minutes."

"A'ight. I'll be here waiting, but I'm not driving my car."

"Whatcha in now?"

"I'm in this dark-colored minivan. I couldn't risk her having the police looking for me in my Camry. That's why I switched cars with my kids' grandmama."

"That was a good idea. I'm gonna swap cars with my wife."

"You coming now? 'Cause I don't know how much longer she's gon' stay in her room."

"I'm leaving out my house right now. Look out for a two thousand eight hunter green Nissan Altima. As a matter of fact, I'm gonna call you when I get within two miles of the hotel."

"A'ight. And if she tries to come out of the hotel before you get here, I'm gon' call you."

"OK. Do that."

I sat there and thought about the conversation Tony and my uncle had just had. To know he wanted my head served to him on a silver platter made me sick to my stomach. It seemed like he wasn't going to rest until he had me the way he wanted me. I wanted to see him suffer at the hands of Walt. I wanted him to be tortured just like I had been, but worse. And I believed in my heart that Walt and Griff would be the men to do it.

Tony sat there on the floor looking severely depressed. I guess he knew his life was about to end, and there was no way of reversing his fate.

I thought about how his children would react when they found out that they'd now lost their father. I knew it would crush their little hearts, and that did bother me, since I would have a hand in their misery. I was wishing I could take those kids and whisk them off with me, so they wouldn't have to stay in this town. So much shit had happened around here, it wasn't even funny. I figured if they came with me, I could show them a better life, but then again, life had a way of throwing people curve balls. So it'd just be my luck that I'd lose them too, since death always seemed to find me.

The ride to my hotel didn't take long. My heart started beating like crazy because I knew there was about to be an all-out war between my uncle and Walt. Griff and Jeff were going to throw their weight around too, so Uncle Lanier was going to be outnumbered three to one.

As Jeff pulled into the parking lot of the hotel, an eerie feeling came over me. There was nothing that looked out of the ordinary when we drove into the parking lot, but I still sensed that something wasn't quite right. I immediately told Jeff to stop. Instead of coming to a complete stop, he slowed down the van and looked at me through the rearview mirror.

Walt turned around and asked me, "What's wrong?"

"Something doesn't feel right."

"Whatcha mean? Explain to me whatcha talking about?"

"I know we suppose to be meeting my uncle here, but I don't feel good about it. I think we should call him back and change the plans."

"What don't you feel good about?" Walt asked.

By this time Jeff had come to a complete stop and had parked the van on the side of the hotel, but away from the other cars. The entire parking lot was lit up with street pole lights, so everything around us was visible.

I sighed heavily. "Look, just take my word for it. When I start getting weird feelings and stuff, something usually goes wrong."

"Well, what do you want us to do?" Walt asked me.

"Let's get out of this parking lot first, and then we can form another plan."

Just as I requested, Jeff turned the van around and headed out of the parking lot. As we were leaving, Tony's cell phone started ringing.

Walt retrieved the phone from his pants pocket and looked down at the caller ID.

"Who is it?" I asked Walt before he could utter one word.

Walt turned toward me and said, "It's your uncle. You think we should answer it?"

"Yeah, you gon' have to, because if you don't, he's gonna think something is wrong."

The phone was on its fourth ring before Walt took the call. He immediately put the phone to Tony's ear.

"Hello," Tony said.

Lanier barked, "What the fuck took you so long to answer your phone?"

"I had the music up, so I didn't hear it ring until now."

"Where the fuck you going?" my uncle asked him.

I immediately peered through the curtains to see if I could locate my uncle. I knew he had to be somewhere in the vicinity, because he could clearly see the van. I looked out both sides of the van, but I still couldn't tell where he was.

"Ask him where he's at," I whispered to Tony.

Tony sounded really nervous, but he managed to repeat the question I instructed him to ask.

"I'm coming into the hotel parking lot from the North Hampton Boulevard entrance, but I see you leaving out on the Military Highway side."

Everybody in the van turned around toward the North Hampton Boulevard entrance of the hotel parking lot, and sure enough, there was my uncle pulling into the opposite side of the parking lot. My heart fell into the pit of my stomach.

"Oh shit! I see him right there," I said, pointing in his direction. He was indeed driving his wife's car, and I could see it as clear as day.

I looked at Walt to see what his next move would be. He looked clueless about how to handle this situation, so I sat back and wondered how this scene would play out.

Walt kept the phone glued to Tony's ear, so he could keep the dialog going while Jeff continued to exit the parking lot from the other side.

"So are you going to turn back around or what?" Lanier asked.

"Yeah, um, er, gi-give me a second," Tony said, stuttering.

"Why you leave anyway? You knew I was coming."

"I left because, er, I didn't want Kira to look out her hotel window and see this van sitting in the parking lot."

"Does she know who the van belongs to?"

"Nah, but I think she saw me pull up when she got out of her cab."

"What made you think that?"

"Because when she got out of her cab, she did a double take, and then she rushed into the hotel."

"Why the fuck didn't you tell me this before? Shit! She might've called the cops."

"Nah, I don't think she did that, because I've been sitting up here ever since I talked to you, and I haven't seen any police patrolling this area."

"You sure?"

"Yeah, I'm sure."

"Well, what you think we should do?" Lanier sounded like he had run out of ideas.

"I think we should park somewhere else, but close, so we can be within walking distance of our cars."

"What the fuck we gon' do when we get on foot? Time is running out for us, so if we gon' do something, we gon' have to do it now. And to begin that process, we need to figure out how the hell we gon' get her out that hotel without anyone seeing us."

"I've been trying to figure that shit out since I got off the phone with you."

"Well, look, let's find a parking spot first, and then we can deal with the other shit after that," Lanier said.

Everybody in the van remained quiet because we didn't want to tip off my uncle that Tony wasn't alone. I guess, since Tony couldn't see exactly where Jeff was driving, he decided to let my uncle suggest where they would both park.

"I see you making a U-turn at the light, so do you want to park over there in that residential area near that basketball court off North Hampton Boulevard?"

Tony looked at Walt, who nodded, giving Tony the green light. "Yeah, that's cool."

"All right. Well, I'll be over there in a second."

"A'ight."

Walt took the phone away from his ear and pressed the end button.

Right after Walt ended the call, Jeff looked at him through the rearview mirror. "You want me to drive over to the residential neighborhood near the basketball court?"

"Yeah."

"What we gon' do when we get over there?" Griff asked.

Walt said, "Jeff, try to beat that nigga over there, so we can jump out the van and wait for him in the cut somewhere."

"A'ight," Jeff said, and then he pressed down on the accelerator.

"You better hurry up, because that red light my uncle is at is getting ready to turn green."

"I'm trying."

When Jeff finally pulled on to the street, I looked around to see if anyone was in the vicinity, but no one was there. Well, at least I didn't see anyone. As soon as Jeff pulled up to the basketball court, Griff and Walt opened the door to get out of the van.

Before Walt closed the sliding door to the van, I asked, "Are you getting ready to take out my uncle now?"

Walt looked at me. "That was the plan."

"Well, do you think I'd be asking too much if you let me torture his ass first? I mean, I want him to feel the same shit he put me through earlier."

Walt looked around to see if my uncle had arrived yet, and when he didn't see any trace of him, he looked back at me and said, "If me and Griff take him hostage, we ain't gon' have a place to put 'im. You see how much space this nigga is taking up," he said, referring to Tony.

I looked at Tony and then back at Walt. "We don't need him anymore, so get rid of him."

"No! No! Please don't kill me!" he pleaded, his voice getting louder and louder with each word that came out of his mouth. If we didn't do something to shut him up, he would've attracted someone's attention, and we didn't need that, especially since we had plans to kidnap my uncle.

A pair of headlights came racing around the corner toward us, and everyone turned around to see who it was.

"Oh shit! My uncle is coming," I said in a panic, paranoia consuming my entire body. He was approximately one hundred and fifty yards from us when we'd first noticed him, and at the speed he was going, it was going to be a matter of seconds before he was right next to us.

Caught totally off guard, Walt and Griff didn't have any time to run for cover and hide behind one of the cars parked near the van, so they both climbed back into the van. As soon as they got back into the van, they closed their doors, looked at each other, and wondered aloud about what their next step was going to be.

The way we were parked, my uncle's car was coming toward us from the back. I watched his car approach from the back window of the van.

Walt scrambled to the back of the van where I was, so he could look out the back window too. "We gotta think of something quick," he said.

"Where is he now?" Griff asked.

"He's pulling up to the back of the van now," Walt told him.

"Yeah, I can see him through my side window," Jeff said.

As Walt and Jeff followed Lanier's every move, I saw Tony moving through my peripheral vision. I turned my head around and looked directly at him. I thought he was trying to ease his way over to the sliding door, but he was only trying to turn on his side. I knew he couldn't be so stupid as to try to scoot his body toward the sliding door, knowing Jeff and Griff would see him. But I'd been taught that you never underestimate anyone, especially those close to you.

Speaking of those close to you, my uncle stopped the car directly behind the minivan. After he turned off the ignition, he got out of the car.

"He's out of the car," I whispered to everyone in the van.

Griff shifted his body, and Jeff pressed the recliner button on the side of his seat so he could lean back. I continued to watch my uncle from the back window as he approached the van. He walked on the left side of the van and headed toward the front. I figured he assumed that Tony was in the driver's seat. I looked toward the front of the van and saw Jeff lay farther back in his seat.

"Walt, whatcha want me to do?" Jeff said. "He's almost at my door."

"Just remain calm and act normal," Walt told him.

"What am I gon' say when he asks me where Tony is?"

Before Walt could answer, my uncle was standing outside the driver's side door. I couldn't see him, but I could hear him clearly.

"Where's Tony?" Lanier asked.

Jeff sat back up in his seat and rolled down his window. "He just ran to the side of that house across the street so he could take a leak."

"I wonder why he didn't tell me he was rolling with somebody. When I talked to him on the phone, he acted like he was rolling solo."

Griff wouldn't look at my uncle. He turned his attention toward the basketball court, which was to his right.

"When he was on the phone with you, I thought you heard us in the background, because me and him was talking the whole time y'all was on the phone."

"Nah, I didn't hear nobody talking."

I heard him take a step backward.

"Which house you said he was by?"

Jeff reached out the window and pointed to a beige-colored ranch-style house to the left of the van. All the lights were out at that house, so it was pretty smart of him to say that was where Tony was trying to take a piss.

I peeped out the left side window of the minivan to see what my uncle was doing. I couldn't see him that good, but I could tell he was getting a little nervous.

Without warning, he yelled, "Hey, Tony. Where you at, man?"

Of course, Tony couldn't answer him because he was tied up in the back of the minivan with me and Walt.

Jeff tried to remain calm, but he knew if Lanier continued to yell, someone who lived in one of the houses in the neighborhood would sure enough look outside their windows to see who was creating all the noise. Jeff knew we didn't need any witnesses, especially since the minivan belonged to him, so he took it upon himself to eliminate the source of the noise. He opened the door, gun in hand.

"Lanier, they trying to kill you! You better run!" Tony blurted out, catching everybody in the van off guard.

Lanier was looking in the direction of the house where he was told Tony was taking a leak. His back was turned to Jeff, so Jeff had the upper hand when he saw Lanier shift his body to turn back around.

Before Lanier could do anything, Jeff was out of the van, and standing before him, his pistol pointed directly at his head. "Nigga, if you say another word, I'ma blow your motherfucking head clean off your shoulders. Now turn your ass back around and put up your hands!"

Just as Lanier turned around and raised his hands, Griff opened his door and hopped out to assist Jeff.

Walt turned his attention to Tony, who was curled up in a fetal position, a dumbfounded expression on his face. He knew he had fucked up royally, and his time on this earth was about to expire. Walt got down on his knees with the gun in hand and started pistol-whipping the hell out of Tony.

Tony screamed, "Owwwww! Please don't kill me! I'm sorry! Please give me another chance."

Blood was flying everywhere. It even got on Walt's face, but Walt acted like it didn't bother him, because he kept pounding Tony with one blow after the next. Tony's face looked really raw, and it became unbearable for me to look at it, so I closed my eyes and placed my face in the palms of my hands.

As Tony's cries got louder and louder, Jeff and Griff grabbed my uncle and marched him around to the side of the minivan to see what was going on.

"What the fuck are you doing?" Jeff asked as soon as he slid the van door open.

"I wanted to teach him a lesson about opening his mouth."

"But why did you do that shit in my van? Do you know how hard it is to clean up blood?"

"Yeah, Walt," Griff said, "he ain't lying. Trying to get rid of bloodstains ain't no easy task."

"Why you ain't just shoot him in his fucking head and be done with it?" Jeff said.

"Good idea." Walt then turned back around, put his gun against Tony's head, and shot him.

Tony's eyes were still open, but his body became still. I knew he was dead.

Uncle Lanier started trying to make deals with Jeff and Griff. "Look, y'all, if y'all let me go, I'll make you very rich."

"That's a fucking lie!" I said. "He ain't even rich himself."

Lanier didn't see me sitting in the back of the minivan, but when he heard my voice, he leaned into the van to see if his ears had played a trick on him. And when he saw my face, he looked like he was about to have a fucking heart attack.

"Surprised to see me, huh?"

While he was at a loss for words, Jeff and Griff started

tying his arms and legs together with duct tape.

"Well, since you ain't got shit to say," I continued, "I might as well tell you that you are about to go on the wildest ride of your life. And when I'm through with your grimy ass, your lame-ass wife gon' be burying you."

"Kira, I know I hurt you, but can you please forgive me? We are family, and nothing should come between that."

I wasn't trying to hear his bullshit. He'd taken me through so much agony and pain, it felt unreal. I still couldn't believe that he'd planned the whole kidnapping thing and participated in torturing me.

Walt took off his shirt and wiped his face with it. There was still a lot of blood near the creases of his eyes and around his nose, which Jeff brought to his attention.

After Jeff and Griff tied up my uncle, they pushed him inside the van, and he fell onto of Tony's limp body. The shit must've scared the hell out of him, because he screamed like a little bitch.

Walt kicked Lanier in his side. "Shut the fuck up!" Then he looked at Jeff and asked him if he had checked my uncle to see if he had a burner on him.

Before Jeff slid back the door, he told Walt, "Yeah, I checked while we were on the other side of the van. He's clean."

"It's probably in his car," I blurted out.

Walt told Griff, "Go check his car and see if he left his burner in there."

"A'ight." Griff dashed off toward Lanier's car.

While Griff searched my uncle's car, Jeff slid the van door closed, got back into the driver's seat, and turned on the ignition. I took it upon myself to look out each window in the back of the van to see if anyone in the neighborhood was peeping out of their front door or windows. Thankfully, I didn't notice anyone watching us.

Once Griff completed his search, he rushed back to the van and hopped into his seat, sounding a little out of breath.

"You all right?" Jeff asked him.

Griff sighed. "Yeah, I'm straight."

"Did you find his pistol?" Walt asked.

"Yeah, I got it right here." Griff showed him Lanier's semi-automatic handgun.

"Walt, you know we gon' have to hurry up and get rid of Tony's body before all his blood soaks into my carpet."

Griff stuck Lanier's gun into the glove compartment. "Yeah, Walt, he's right. We gon' have to get rid of his body ASAP."

"Where you think we should put him?" Walt asked.

"Let's leave him in the same spot where we put his girl," Griff suggested.

"Nah, that won't be a good idea," Jeff said. "It would be really stupid to go back to the same area where we dumped off one body, and then turn around to do the same shit again. For all we know, somebody could've seen this van, so if we chance it and go back out there, we would really become suspect."

"He's right," I said. "That makes a lot of sense."

"So think of another spot then."

"Stick him in the trunk of his car," I said.

Walt shook his head. "Nah, that'll be too risky."

As Jeff put the van in gear and drove away from the basketball court, I looked out the back of the van window at Lanier's wife's car. Knowing she was going to call 9-1-1 and report her husband missing in the morning made me think about how a person could be here one day and gone the next. Life had a funny way of throwing stones at you. I was just hoping I would be able to duck each one thrown at me from this day forward.

By the time Jeff got back to the main road, Griff and Walt had both figured out where they were going to dump Tony's body. I didn't quite agree with their decision because of the risk they were going to take, but since I didn't have a say in the matter, I let it go. I prayed to God that everything would work out, so I could walk away from this thing and get back out of town as quickly as possible.

I watched my uncle as he lay on the floor of the van. I noticed that he wouldn't look at me, so I made it my business to torment the hell out of him. "You can't look at me, can you?" I asked, but of course he ignored me.

Walt said, "He knows he fucked up. That's why he can't look at you."

While Walt was talking to me, I couldn't help but look at the blood that was drying on his face. It made him look really sadistic. I began to look at him in another light. I was beginning to see this other person. He wasn't the man my mother used to be with when I was a child.

Back then he was a sweetheart, and I could tell that he had a heart. He used to treat me like I was his biological daughter, and he still did, but for some reason I didn't see that glow in his eyes anymore. Tonight his eyes were dark, and I didn't like it. So, instead of commenting on what he'd said about my uncle, I turned my attention to the left side window and watched the streetlights and the cars as we drove by, on our way to complete my mission for revenge.

STREET CREDIBILITY

The dumpsite for Tony's body was the Pretty Lake section of Ocean View, which was a neighborhood off Shore Drive in Norfolk. I'd always known Ocean View to be plagued with gang violence and heavy drug trafficking. Police were known to frequent this part of Norfolk, so I was leery from the beginning when they suggested that we dump Tony's body there.

I sat back in the van and plotted a getaway just in case the police ran up on us. When Jeff stopped the van at the lake on Third Bay Street, I climbed into the seat beside Walt so I could make my escape if their plans were derailed.

Jeff got out of the van first, and Griff and Walt followed. Each of them checked their gloves to see if they were intact before they moved Tony's body out of the van.

Walt instructed me to keep an eye on Lanier. "If he moves one inch, don't hesitate to shoot his ass!" he told me.

"I won't." I still had the gun Walt had given me earlier, so I was ready for whatever. My uncle looked at me like he was surprised, but he wasn't in a position to say one word.

Between watching Walt and the guys remove Tony's body from the van, and trying to keep an eye on my uncle, my mind was running in circles. I also made it my business to watch my back. I refused to let a police officer run up on this van while I was holding my uncle at gunpoint. We would have a fucking shootout right here in Ocean View, if they thought I was gonna let them take me downtown in handcuffs. No way!

"Damn, nigga!" Jeff said to Griff. "Can you hold his legs better than that?"

"What the fuck you think I'm doing?"

"It feels like I'm carrying him by myself."

Griff snapped. "Man, shut the fuck up complaining! You act like you're putting in more work than me and Walt."

"Nigga, you the one that needs to shut the fuck up! You been complaining since we picked up Walt and homegirl."

"Look, both of y'all need to cut that shit out! Let's take care of our business and get the fuck out of here before somebody sees us and calls the police."

"He's right, y'all." I peered out of the van at the apartment buildings in the area. "Because as soon as someone hears y'all voices, they're going to look out their windows. And y'all don't want the heat that comes from that."

Jeff chimed back in. "Tell this nigga to handle his part and I won't complain no more."

Walt looked at them both as they all scrambled to carry Tony's body toward the lake behind the apartment buildings. "Can we just finish what we started without y'all saying another word to each other?"

"Just tell this nigga to do his part, Walt, and I won't have no beef," Jeff said.

Walt refused to jump on anyone's side. He wasn't that type of guy. He just wanted shit to run smooth, no matter what it was. So when I saw him switch places with Jeff to relieve him of some of the burden, I knew he was tired of hearing their mouths.

As I watched my uncle, and occasionally looked outside the van to see if anyone was watching us, I thought about how badly I wanted to get Kasey. *Her body should be thrown in this lake along with Tony's.* I just couldn't believe how she'd gotten away from us just like that. God must've been on her side and had a plan for her, because if it was up to me, that bitch would be expired by now.

While I was deep in thought I heard a soft whisper calling my name. It kind of scared me a bit because my mind was somewhere else. When I tuned into the voice and realized it was my uncle calling me, I gave him the nastiest expression I could muster, and then I asked him what the hell he wanted.

"Please can you find it in your heart to forgive?" He kept the volume of his voice down, because he refused to let Walt hear him talk to me. He knew it would be hell to pay if he did.

"Forgive you, and you almost killed me? Are you fucking crazy?" I lashed out, not even realizing how loud I'd gotten.

Walt yelled at me from the lake to be quiet, and he was about two hundred feet away from me.

"Kira, I know you must think I'm crazy, but I turned into a madman after I lost Nikki. I had just lost my mother to that Hispanic guy from D.C. who was after Nikki. So can't you feel my pain?"

If I was a dragon, fire would have spewed out of my mouth every time I opened it. "You act like you're the only one who lost someone. Grandma meant more to me than you would ever know. She was like my mother, so when I found out she had been murdered, a huge part of my heart felt like it was yanked out of my body. And as far as Nikki is concerned, it hurts me to know that she's gone too, but I've got to tell you that she wasn't the angel y'all made her out to be at her funeral." I waved the pistol Walt gave me back and forth in his face. "Right before we went to Texas I noticed that something about Nikki had changed. But I figured she was just going through a rough time because we had just lost our grandmother. So when we got to Texas, everything about her did a hundred-and-eighty-degree turn. She started competing against me when it came to certain things, she talked about me to other stylists behind my back, and she fucked my fiancé without me knowing."

"No, not Nikki. She wouldn't do that to you. She loved you like a sister. She used to tell me how she looked up to you."

"Shut the fuck up, Uncle Lanier. You don't know what the fuck you are talking about. That precious little daughter of yours took me through more shit than any of my enemies. She tried to sabotage everything I put my hands on. And you want to know something else? Your little angel helped set up a few women to get killed back in Texas."

"That can't be. Nikki wasn't like that. She wouldn't hurt a soul."

"That's a motherfucking lie. Nikki helped my fiancé rape and kill innocent women for his own sick gratification. She went to nightclubs and lured these women to him so they could all get in a threesome, and then those poor women's lives would end soon thereafter. And you want to know something else?"

He just continued to look at me dumbfounded.

"Nikki was killed because she was involved in some scandalous shit. I was there when the guy shot and killed her and my ex-fiancé, and I couldn't do anything to help her."

My uncle lay there on the floor and shook his head in disbelief.

I knew it was hard for him to swallow that pill, but it was the truth. His daughter had moved to Houston with me and lost her fucking mind. I didn't know who the hell she was anymore when she flipped the script on me.

Thankfully, all that shit was behind me now, and when I took care of him and left this godforsaken place, this chapter in my life would finally be closed.

The conversation between my uncle and me didn't stop after I blew his mind with the story about his little girl helping Fatu' kill all those women in Houston. He tried to talk my head off about letting him go. He promised that, if I let him go, he wouldn't go to the homicide detectives in Houston and tell them what I told him about Nikki's murder. He also promised me that he would give me all the money he saved up for his retirement.

I looked at him and told him that I didn't need his money. I honestly wanted to tell him that I had over two million dollars back in Anguilla, where I now lived, but I didn't want to let on how well-off I was, or that the place I called home was out of the country. He was a fucking traitor to me, so I couldn't trust him with that type of information. It was bad enough that I told him the truth about his daughter. But, hey, I figured since he was about to lose his life, it wouldn't matter one way or another. I mean, it wasn't like he could pick up the phone and call the cops on me. He had one foot in the grave, and the other was treading on thin ice, so I was all right anyway I looked at it.

I looked at the time on the dashboard of the van. It was eleven fifteen P.M. Time was flying by at the speed of a comet, and we still had one more job to do before we could call it quits. I looked over at the lake and saw the men struggling to dump Tony's body in the water.

I heard Walt telling Griff and Jeff that they needed to tie something heavy to his legs so his body could sink to the bottom of the lake.

"We can't have anyone finding him right after we dump him in this lake because his body resurfaced to the top of the water," Walt said.

"What about this old car tire? You think this could work?" Griff asked.

Walt hesitated and then said, "I don't know. Bring it here and let me check it out."

While Griff carried the tire to Walt, Jeff said, "Hey, I see a couple of sandbags over here."

Walt turned in his direction. "Now that'll work." He instructed Jeff to bring the bags to him.

I watched Jeff carry both sandbags to Walt, and then he set them on the ground near Tony's body.

Ten minutes later I wanted to ask them why the hell they hadn't gotten rid of Tony's body yet. I wanted to get the hell out of there.

"Kira, can you please find it in your heart to forgive me? I swear if you spare my life, I will forever be indebted to you," my uncle said again, taking my focus off Walt and the other two guys.

"Why do you keep asking me the same fucking question? Do you know that I don't even feel sorry for you? So stop wasting your breath, because ain't nothing gonna change. You are going to get dealt with as soon as Walt takes care of Tony. That's it, and that's all."

Tears started falling from my uncle's eyes.

In all the days of my life, I had never seen this twenty-year army veteran who'd fought in Vietnam shed one tear. Growing up around him, he'd always had a hard exterior, so to see him about to have an emotional breakdown really got me to think about this situation from another perspective. Either he was really sorry for what he did to me, or he was afraid of dying.

"Remember when you were seven years old and you and your mother came to my house to celebrate Nikki's third birthday?"

I sucked my teeth. "Yeah, so what?"

"Do you remember we were all in the house eating and you decided to go take a swim in the pool and almost drowned?"

Getting aggravated, I said, "What point are you trying to make?"

"Do you remember that day?" He pressed the issue.

"Yes, I remember."

"Do you remember who saved your life and performed CPR on you after you were pulled from the pool unconscious?"

I sucked my teeth once again. "Where are you going with this?"

"All I'm trying to say is, there was no other adult in my house who knew how to perform CPR, so I immediately pulled you from the pool and saved your life. You were unconscious for three whole minutes. Everybody there, including your mother, thought we'd lost you, but I was determined to bring you back. You were like a daughter to me, and I wasn't about to let your mother bury you at such a young age. You were her only child, and you were my only niece, so letting you leave us like that wasn't an option. Your life was in my hands then, and now my life is in your hands. So I'm begging you to let me live."

My uncle's words started to sink in. He was right. My

life was in his hands that day, and he did save me. What was bugging me out right now was that I held the cards to either end his or save it. And the more I thought about it, the more I started to understand his position.

"Kira, let's end this deadly cycle right now. We already lost your mother, your grandmother, your husband, and Nikki. No one else needs to die. So please have a change of heart so we can walk away from this thing," he said, and then he fell silent.

I looked him dead in his eyes and they were very glassy. Something on the inside of me wanted to reach out and hug him because of the hurt he was going through. But then the other part of me wanted to kick him like Walt had done earlier. I just couldn't erase what he'd put me through. And every time I tried to put it out of my mind, it resurfaced.

Finally Walt, Jeff, and Griff tied both sandbags to Tony's body and threw him into the lake. When his body hit the water, I heard a big splash. I couldn't see where they threw his body, but I knew he was in there. I then saw them standing by the lake looking into the water. I assumed they were waiting until his body sunk to the bottom, because they didn't make another move.

"Kira, please let me go. Don't let Walt be the one to tear the rest of our family apart. You've got the control in this situation."

"No, I don't. It's out of my hands now. After I escaped you, I went to Walt and he said that he was going to handle everything for me." I turned my attention back to Walt, Jeff, and Griff.

"Did you ever find out the real reason your mother left Walt?"

Shocked by my uncle's question, I turned my attention back to him. "What?"

"Did your mother ever tell you the real reason why she left Walt?"

"No."

"Had you ever asked her about it?"

"Well, all I asked her was why we were moving back to Grandma's house."

"And what did she say?"

"She never really gave me a straight answer. All she said was that they were separating, so we had to move out. But Walt told me that it was you and grandma that broke them up."

"I hate to break it to you, but that was a lie. When your mother started dating Walt, he was a pimp, and she didn't know it until after y'all moved into his place. And before your mother knew it, he had her strung out on drugs and tricking on Church Street."

"Nah, I don't believe that. My mother would not have ever stood on the streets and sold her body. She was too high-class for that. She wore more designer name brands than most celebrities on TV."

"That period in her life started after she left Walt and entered rehab."

"Rehab? My mother never went to a rehab!" I roared, jumping to her defense.

I didn't remember her ever going to a rehab center,

and I sure as hell didn't remember her tricking on Church Street. However, I did remember her coming late at night to Walt's house, and Walt asking her where his money was. I always heard her tell him that it was in her purse, but I never thought anything of it. I chalked up those conversations to her either borrowing money from him, or her taking money out of his wallet without him knowing it.

"Kira, do you remember when she used to leave you at grandma's house every other night and tell you she had to go to work?"

"Yeah."

"Where do you think she was going? She wasn't clocking in at the nightclub doing bartending work like she had you believing. She was out on the corner working for Walt."

I shook my head in disbelief. "I'm sorry, but I don't believe it."

"Well, do you remember the morning your mother picked you up and you asked her why she had that black eye? And she told you she got into a fight with a guy who tried to mug her when he was leaving work."

I sat back and thought back to that particular morning, and I did remember that. As a matter of fact, he and my grandmother were both there encouraging her to stay at the house with them. "Yeah, I do remember that," I told him.

"Walt was the one who hit your mother, Kira. He was very abusive and controlling toward her. He was the guy who beat her up that night before she came to pick you up."

"Why?"

"Because she told him she didn't want to live her life like that anymore, and that she wanted to get off the streets. But he wasn't trying to hear that. He wanted her to continue working for him. And when your mother stood up to him and told him that night was her last night selling her body, he punched her in her face and tried to hurt her pretty badly. As soon as I saw her face, I went to his house with my gun in my hand, pointed it directly at his head, and threatened to pull the motherfucking trigger if he ever put his hands on her again."

"What did he do?"

"He couldn't do shit. He was alone, and I didn't give him a chance to get his gun from inside his house. So I pretty much had him on his knees. But now the tables have turned. He got me on my knees now. So I know he's itching to get me back. I saw it in his face when the other guy brought me around the side of the van."

"Maybe he is, but I don't think no one wanted you more than me."

"Nah, I don't think so. When I pulled my gun out on him that day, I tested his manhood, and he didn't like that one bit. He has had a personal vendetta against me for many years, and he's not going to be happy until he gets back at me."

Hearing my uncle tell me what I had always wanted to know was disturbing. But what really messed up my head was how I'd confided in a man who had no respect for my mother and damn near took her life. He'd introduced her to drugs and forced her to be a fucking prostitute. I couldn't believe how he had pulled the wool over my eyes all this damn time. How grimy could he be?

I wanted to confront him at that very moment with this shit, and put him on blast, but this wasn't the right time. Plus, I didn't know how he'd react. I had never seen Walt's bad side until I saw him pistol-whip the hell out of Tony. He looked menacing, and if he unleashed that same demon on me, I wouldn't know how to handle it.

I sat there for a moment and tried to figure out how I would play out this scene. I was still upset with my uncle and wanted his head on a chopping block, but at the same time, the thought of what Walt had done to my mother, and the fact that he had fooled me all this time sent my blood pressure through the roof. I wanted his head on the chopping block alongside my uncle's. But I knew I couldn't have it both ways, so I had to figure out which one deserved to be there more.

Tony's body must have finally sunk to the bottom of the lake, because Walt, Griff, and Jeff began to walk back toward the van. From the moment they took their first step in my direction, my heart started beating out of control. My uncle couldn't see them, but he heard their steps, so when he started talking to me again, there was some urgency in his voice.

"They coming for me, Kira. So what's it going to be?"

I thought for a second about my uncle. It was already etched in stone that Walt would take his life, and I still didn't have one ounce of sympathy for him. Everything he'd done to me warranted the plans Walt and I had for him. But by the same token, I wrestled with the thought of what Walt took my mother through back when we lived with him. I knew I couldn't get both of them the way I wanted, so I had to make a choice, and I also knew that I needed to do it quickly.

I looked at my uncle and said, "If I help you get away, are we gonna end this on a good note and go our separate ways?"

He tried to respond to my question, but I interrupted him before he could utter one word. "I don't want to hear you breathe my fucking name for no reason at all. After tonight, I don't exist anymore. We are no longer related. I am dead as far as you're concerned, so don't try to find me. I don't care if you're on your deathbed, just leave well enough alone. And if I find out the Houston homicide detectives are looking for me, then you will have hell to pay. Do you understand me?"

He nodded.

I turned around and looked back in the direction of Walt and the other guys. I figured I had about thirty-five seconds to do or say whatever I needed to say to my uncle before they reached the van. I reached inside my handbag and grabbed the small utility knife I had attached to my nail clipper. Since his hands were tied behind his back, I leaned down and placed the knife in his hands. When I sat back up, I looked into his face and noticed how his expression had changed. I could tell that his spirits had lifted. "Use that to cut yourself loose," I whispered to him.

Unfortunately for him he couldn't respond. Walt, Griff, and Jeff were already within arm's reach of the van. When they grabbed the door to climb back into the van, my uncle and I both changed our expressions.

"Is he behaving?" Walt wanted to know right after he climbed into the van.

I cracked a half-smile and told him I had everything under control.

As Jeff started up the ignition and drove the van away from the lake, I started to climb back into the last of seat of the van, but I decided against it this time, and stayed where I was, which was in the middle seat.

Walt sat beside me, while my uncle lay on the floor. He placed his feet four inches away from my uncle's face. "I ought to spit on you and kick you in your motherfucking face! The sight of you makes me sick to my stomach. And I can't wait to get you in a place where no one will hear you while I torture your ass to death."

"Where are you taking him?" I asked.

Griff suggested that we take him to this abandoned dumpsite in the Berkeley section of Norfolk, so when we were done with his body, we could just leave him there.

Griff said, "No one is going to find him for at least a couple of months." Then he smiled. "Probably longer than that."

I didn't comment at all. My main focus was to figure out an escape plan for my uncle before Walt and the rest of the guys made him into mincemeat. I knew that if I tried to change Walt's mind about killing Lanier, he'd probably look at me and laugh. The other guys probably would laugh in my face too. Not after he'd witnessed Walt kill Tony. Plus, he'd witnessed all three of them dispose of his body.

I was an accessory to three counts of murder, and not only that, but I'd confessed and told my uncle that I'd witnessed Nikki's murder, so I had more to lose than anybody. But I was still willing to set him free if I could kill the bastard who had hurt my mother.

DOWN TO THE WIRE

The first ten minutes of the ride to Berkeley was pretty quiet until Walt started tormenting my uncle, kicking him a couple times in the stomach, talking a lot of shit to him, and reminding him that he planned to beat him when he got to the location.

I noticed the fear in my uncle's eyes grow. A small part of me felt sorry for him. If I didn't get him out of this van before we got to that dumpsite in Berkeley, my chances of helping him escape would be gone. Time was running out.

I looked down at my uncle while Walt continued to badger him. I couldn't talk out loud, so I moved my mouth in hopes that he could read my lips. I instructed him to cut off the ropes from around his wrists.

He looked at me like he didn't understand, so I made a few hand gestures. I placed my finger against my wrist and moved it back and forth like I was slicing something. He got my drift then.

Meanwhile, Jeff informed us that he needed to stop and get some gas.

Walt didn't think it was a good idea, but when Jeff stressed to him that they wouldn't make it to the dumpsite unless he stopped, he said, "Look, I don't care what you do, just as long as you don't stop at a gas station that's crowded with people."

"A'ight," Jeff replied.

I looked straight to the front of the van and noticed that the gas light was on. Then I looked back down at my uncle and started mouthing instructions to him again. I told him to get ready, and he seemed to understand.

My heart started beating uncontrollably. It felt like I was the one trying to escape, not my uncle.

Griff said, "Man, I'm so glad you're stopping, because I gotta take a shit really bad."

"We don't have time for that, Griff," Walt snapped. "You gon' have to tighten up them butt cheeks and hold back, 'cause we got a mission to complete."

Griff turned around in his seat. "I understand what you're saying, Walt, but I ain't gon' be able to hold this shit any longer. I've been holding this shit since I left your house."

Walt shook his head. "Nah, I can't let you get out this van."

"Yo, Walt, I ain't bullshitting you. My stomach is killing me right now. And if I don't take care of it real soon, I'm gon' end up shitting on myself."

Jeff started cracking up with laughter.

"Griff, you know this ain't how we conduct business. And, Jeff, you know you should've stopped and got some motherfucking gas before you picked me up. All this stopping shit is for amateurs, and I ain't no motherfucking amateur. So y'all need to get y'all shit together."

"I got my shit together," Jeff said as he pulled into a BP service station off Chesapeake Boulevard, a quarter mile from the Five Points intersection. "If we weren't riding all over the Tidewater area, I wouldn't have to stop and get gas. I had a little over a quarter tank, so that was enough for the trip out Huntersville, Military Highway, and that spot out at Virginia Beach. But when you added Barraud Park and fucking Ocean View, that kind of took it to the limit."

When Jeff pulled up to a gas pump and shut off the ignition, Griff immediately opened the passenger door and hopped out of his seat without saying one word. He shut the door behind him and raced off to use the service station restroom.

Jeff burst into laughter as he watched Griff race toward the store. "I'ma laugh my ass off if that nigga shits on himself."

Walt wasn't in the mood. "Can you hurry up and pump the gas so we can get the fuck out of here?"

Jeff looked back at Walt before he got out of the van and assured him that he was on it. Then he got out of the van and closed the door.

I looked back at my uncle. He was looking toward the van door. I could tell he was trying to avoid eye contact with Walt as much as possible.

Walt sat in the chair next to me with an evil expression on his face, staring at Jeff until he disappeared behind the door of the service station.

While Walt's attention was on Jeff, my uncle managed to cut the rope off his wrists. I watched him through my peripheral vision. I didn't want to focus my attention on him, because Walt would have caught on to what he was doing.

Griff was in the bathroom stall almost one hundred and fifty feet away from the van, while Jeff was in the store paying for the gas. *This is the perfect opportunity.*

I looked through the window of the service station and noticed that there were two people ahead of Jeff. I figured I only had about a minute and a half before the window of opportunity would be closed.

Walt's focus was on everything around us. Every time someone walked by the van, or a car pulled up to a gas pump, he made it his business to turn around to see what they were doing.

I could tell that he felt uneasy and paranoid because of everything going on around him. This was the perfect opportunity for me to execute my plan.

I still had the gun in my hand from when he gave it to me earlier. I pulled back on the hammer very lightly, so he wouldn't hear it, and then raised it and pointed it at the side of Walt's head. "Don't say a word unless I tell you to!"

Walt tried to turn his head around to look at me, but I pressed the gun against his temple and told him not to move.

He chuckled like he found what I was doing very amusing. "What's going on, baby girl? You don't like being on my team anymore?" He grinned.

"Just hand me your gun."

As Walt handed me his gun, Lanier brought his arms from around his back and pulled himself up into a sitting position. His eyes grew wide at seeing Lanier free. Once I had Walt's gun in my hand, I immediately stuck it down into the waistband of my shorts.

"I can't believe you helping this motherfucker after all that shit he put you through earlier. You told me he tried to kill you, so what the fuck is wrong with you?"

I was nervous, and Walt could sense it, because he made the comment that if I gave him his gun back that very moment, he would act like what I did never happened. As much as I wanted to do just that, I knew he wasn't going to let me off the hook that easy.

According to Lanier, he'd whipped my mother's ass because she tried to sabotage his plans for her, so why wouldn't he do the same shit to me? Not only that, but he hated when someone pointed a gun at him and didn't pull the trigger. Lanier had done it to him years ago, and now I was doing the exact same thing, so I knew he wouldn't have mercy on me.

"I want you to get out of the van very slowly," I told Walt.

He leaned forward, grabbed the door handle, and slid the door back slowly.

"Don't open it up too wide."

He pulled the door back halfway. "Is this good?"

"Yeah, that's good. Now get out very slowly." I continued to point the gun directly at him.

While he was exiting the van, I looked over his shoulders to see if Jeff had gotten to the register and paid for his gas yet, and sure enough, he was at the register handing the cashier his money. In less than ten seconds Jeff would be right back at the van.

"Hurry up! You're moving too slowly." I pushed Walt in the back. I must have thrown him off balance, because he stumbled a bit when his feet hit the ground.

By then my uncle had managed to break free of the duct tape around his ankles, so he was ready to go. Without saying a word, he climbed into the driver's seat and started up the ignition.

I immediately looked at him and asked, "What the hell you doing?"

"I'm about to get us out of here! Now hurry up and slam the door closed!"

Right when I grabbed on the door handle to slam the door shut, Jeff reappeared and gave me a puzzled look. I was sure his little mind was wondering why Walt was standing outside the van, not to mention, why his van's ignition had been started when he'd shut it off before he'd stepped out of the van to pay for the gas.

Walt yelled, "They trying to get away!"

I assume Jeff had a delayed reaction. He started sprinting after us only after Lanier yelled, "Close the door!" and sped out of the service station, and into oncoming traffic on Chesapeake Boulevard.

From the back window I saw Jeff pull out his gun and aim it at us as, but for some reason, he didn't fire.

I screamed at the top of my voice when Lanier sped in front of this eighteen-wheeler, almost causing us to get sideswiped.

The truck driver pressed his hand against his horn and held it down for dear life. The shit scared the hell out of me. The sound of his horn echoed in my ears, causing me to cringe, and I fell down to my knees, knocking the gun out of my hand to the floor, and it slid underneath the front passenger seat.

I crawled toward the back of that seat and reached my hand underneath it, trying to feel my way around until I located it. It was very difficult to put my hands on it because of how fast my uncle was driving.

When he sped through the red light at the intersection of Five Points, I honestly thought he had lost his motherfucking mind. I heard at least four different car horns blowing. I yelled, "If you don't slow down, you're gonna get us killed!"

"I'm just trying to get away from those niggas as quickly as possible," he yelled, panting.

I finally located the gun, grabbed it, and removed it from underneath the chair. When I tried to stand, I felt the van jerk a couple of times. "What's wrong? Why is the van jerking?" I asked as I sat back on the chair.

Right when he was about to tell me what was wrong, I had already figured it out, because the van's ignition turned off completely. We were coasting on fumes, and then after the van moved a few more feet, it stopped.

We were only one block away from where we'd left Walt and Jeff. They both knew the van was on empty, so we couldn't get very far. There was no doubt in my mind that they were already en route to kill us both.

We had reached the ramp to jump on Highway 64. We knew we couldn't take the chance of running away from the highway to get into the nearby neighborhood called Norview, because we could run right into Walt and Jeff. So we got out of the van and fled on foot toward the traffic on the interstate, praying we wouldn't get hit.

My uncle didn't look back once as he ran down the side ramp of the highway. Cars blew their horns at us when they drove by. I tried my best to keep up with my uncle, but I couldn't.

"Get the hell out of the way!" one driver yelled.

When I heard gunfire, I looked back and noticed Walt and Jeff were both on our tails. Jeff was the only one with a pistol, so he didn't hesitate to bust two shots at us. I was tired of running, but when I heard those shots, I got a burst of energy from out of nowhere.

"Uncle Lanier, they're behind us, and they're shooting!" I yelled.

"Shoot back at them!"

Now I didn't know how to aim a gun and fire a shot at someone while they were in pursuit, and I wasn't about to stop and try it, so I kept it moving.

"Shit!" I said, realizing I had just lost the gun I had placed in the waistband of my shorts. I started to stop to pick it up, but Walt and Jeff were gaining yards on me.

"They're gaining on us!" I screamed. I was in bad shape. My heart was beating uncontrollably, and I was running out of breath.

"You better come on," Lanier yelled back. Saving me from them was the last thing on his mind. He was more concerned about himself, and he didn't try to hide it.

I don't know how, but we ran all the way down Highway 64 until we got to the overpass. Then we ran down a small hill of grass to get to the street underneath the highway, which was Virginia Beach Boulevard.

When I reached the bottom of the hill, I heard voices behind me. I looked back and saw Walt and Jeff at the top of the fucking hill. At that very moment, my life flashed in front of me, and this time around I saw my life come to an end in that cloud. I seriously wanted to stop in my tracks and surrender. At least then I could finally be put out of my misery.

But then something inside me lit up and told me to save myself, and after this last time, I wouldn't ever have to run for my life again. I guess that was all I needed to know, because I put one foot in front of the other and sprinted toward the underpass.

I turned the corner to travel under the underpass, and my uncle had vanished. Fear engulfed my entire body. I didn't know if I was coming or going, but I kept on running.

It was extremely dark under the tunnel, but that really didn't matter to me, because my mission was to get as far away as I could from these niggas. They were after my blood, and I wasn't about to let that happen.

While I was running underneath this dark underpass, going in the direction of Newtown Road, I heard a voice. It scared me to death. I thought it was some homeless person trying to get my attention, but when I realized the person knew my name, I stopped in my tracks.

"Kira, I'm up here," my uncle said.

I was out of breath, yet I somehow mustered up the energy to climb up the slanted, cement wall. When I got to the top, I saw my uncle hiding inside a little box-shaped compartment right under the highway above us.

"Where is the other gun?"

"I dropped it when I was running down the fucking highway, but I still got this one," I replied in a low whisper. I showed him the gun with the silencer.

He took the gun out of my hand and clutched it in his.

Not even a second passed before Walt and Jeff came running around the wall of the underpass. Jeff still had his gun.

My uncle and I were sitting in a small crawl space at the top of the underpass, and those two bastards had to run past us to get out. He leaned into my ear and whispered, "You know that if we don't get them now, they gon' keep coming after us?"

I nodded, not wanting to make any noise. I couldn't afford to draw any attention to us. Right now we had an advantage because we were the predator stalking our prey.

"Stay right here. I'll be right back." Uncle Lanier stood and snuck quietly down the wall, so he could catch Walt and Jeff before they were able to pass us.

I watched him closely as he tiptoed toward them without being heard. When he got close enough he aimed the gun at them and pulled the trigger. I couldn't hear the shots because of the silencer, but when Jeff collapsed on the ground beside Walt and didn't move again, I knew he had gotten hit and was probably dead.

Walt must've seen Jeff fall to the ground, because he turned around and looked back for a brief second, and then he started running faster.

I thought he might have stopped to pick up Jeff's gun, but he must've figured out that would've made him an easy target.

My uncle hurried to catch Walt like he was in the fifty-yard dash, but I couldn't see which direction they ran because of where I was sitting.

It was pitch-dark under the underpass, but I noticed that cars slowed down as they rode by Jeff's body. I saw one woman on her cell phone talking to someone. I didn't know who she was talking to, but it would just be my luck if she was calling the police.

I knew it was time for me to get the hell out of Dodge. I got up from where I was sitting and walked down the wall as quickly as possible. Cars were still slowing down when they passed Jeff's body, so I covered my face to prevent anyone from seeing me when I got close to his body.

I started walking in the opposite direction from where my uncle and Walt had run, but then I heard a car squealing its tires, and a loud crash followed.

Without thinking about it twice, I turned around and ran toward the scene. On my way to see what had happened, I had to step over Jeff's body. As I did, I quickly snatched up his gun and then kept moving.

When I reached the corner of Kempsville Road and Virginia Beach Boulevard, I noticed that the traffic was congested in front of the Chevrolet dealership less than a half a block away. It became apparent that someone had gotten hit, because a crowd of people had gathered around in a circle.

I wanted to know what really happened, so I decided to go over and check it out myself. As I made my way down toward the scene, I noticed someone running toward me. I shoved Jeff's gun into my pocket and tried to act normal. I took a deep breath and looked straight ahead.

Then I realized that it was my uncle. I was so relieved.

He was panting very hard. "Come on and turn around," he said.

"What happened down there? And where is Walt?"

He grabbed my arm and turned me around. "We can't go back near that other guy's body, so let's walk toward Sentara Leigh Hospital."

As my uncle and I marched through the intersection of Kempsville Road and Virginia Beach Boulevard, I noticed he was deep in thought. But that didn't deter me from asking him again what had happened, and where was Walt.

"He's dead."

"What? Did he get hit by a car?"

"I shot him in his leg first, and when I tried to hit him again, he tried to get away from me by running across the street. He got hit head-on by this white guy driving a Ford F-250 truck."

"So what did you do with the gun?"

"I threw it down the sewer near the car dealership."

"You didn't let anybody see you doing it, did you?"

"No. I looked both ways before I dropped it."

I wanted to fall down on my knees and thank God. My life had been spared once again. No matter what situation I got into, God always had my back and made a way for me to get out of it, and for that I was truly grateful.

As we walked down Kempsville Road, I wondered how this night was going to end. Were my uncle and I going to remain distant and move on with our lives as I had planned? Or were we going to bury the hatchet and try to forgive one another? At this point in the game, it didn't matter to me, because either way I looked at it, I was going back out of the country, so he would never see me again.

"Ahh shit! I just thought about something," he said and came to a complete stop.

I stopped in my tracks and asked him what was wrong.

"Do you realize our fingerprints are all over Jeff's van, and he's lying underneath the underpass dead?"

Suddenly, once again, I was back at square one. "So whatcha think we should do?"

"I don't know, but we're gonna have to do something, because not only are our fingerprints in there, but Tony's blood is too. So when the homicide detectives dust the van for prints and take the blood samples from the rug, we could get charged with murder, and we'll never see daylight again."

"How can I go to jail and I ain't killed nobody?"

"The police don't know that."

"You can tell 'em I didn't have shit to do with none of this stuff!" I screeched.

"Kira, you're just as guilty as I am. You were there for Tony's murder too."

"So what? You started all of this bullshit! I didn't ask to be kidnapped and tortured to death."

He took a step toward me and gave me a sinister look. "So whatcha think . . . I'm just gon' take all the heat just like that?"

Looking directly into my uncle's eyes, I could see how serious he was. He wasn't about to compromise, even though he was the one who had started all this shit. I now realized I had fucked up by helping this ungrateful motherfucker escape. I had tried to end the deadly cycle of my family members getting killed because of something I was involved in, but now I saw that this was something I couldn't control.

Without even blinking, I stuck my right hand inside my pocket, eased out Jeff's gun, and aimed it at my uncle's stomach. "You're gonna have to!" I said in a menacing tone, pulling the trigger twice.

He collapsed to the ground with his eyes wide open, bleeding all over the sidewalk. I stepped across him and walked back in the direction of Virginia Beach Boulevard.

When I reached the intersection, I noticed how congested it was. Police vehicles were everywhere. I saw two vans from the Office of the Chief Medical Examiner and three forensic teams. And one officer stood in the intersection and directed the traffic in both directions. I lifted my head up as high as I could and walked by him like my shit didn't stink.

My mission was to find the nearest pay phone. After walking two blocks, I found one. I immediately made an international collect call to Donovan's cell phone. Boy, was I happy to hear his voice when he answered on the first ring.

"Yes, I'll accept the charges," he said. And then when the operator cleared the line for him to speak, he said, "Baby, where are you? I've been calling your phone all night, and it kept going straight to voice mail."

I took a deep breath and exhaled. "Listen, baby, I know you were worried, and as soon as I see you, I'm going to tell you everything that happened to me."

"Tell me now," he insisted.

"Donovan, please just let me get back home first."

"OK, baby. Come on home."

"I am."

After we hung up with one another, I jumped in a taxi and headed straight to the hotel to pick up my belongings, and then I had the driver drop me off at the Norfolk International Airport. I was leaving this country and never coming back.

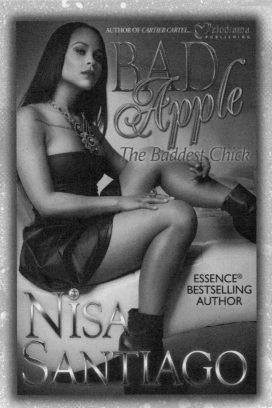

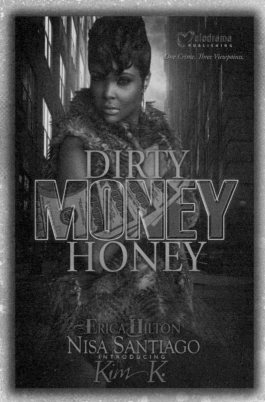

FROM MISTRESS TO WIFEY

FROM THE ORIGINAL PUBLISHER OF WIFEY

ESSENCE® BESTSELLING AUTHOR
ERICA HILTON

WIFEY: FROM MISTRESS TO WIFEY
BY ERICA HILTON
NOVEMBER 8, 2011

TEAM MELODRAMA

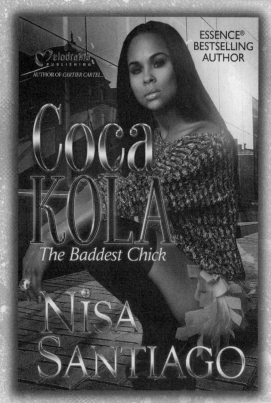

ESSENCE® BESTSELLING AUTHOR

Melodrama PUBLISHING
AUTHOR OF *CARTIER CARTEL...*

Coca KOLA
The Baddest Chick

NISA SANTIAGO

**COCA KOLA
BY NISA SANTIAGO
MARCH 13, 2012**

TEAM MELODRAMA

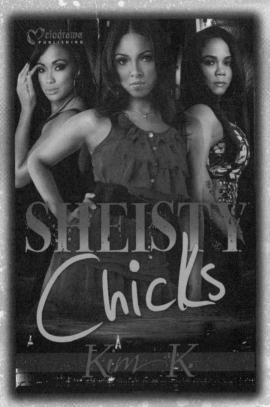

SHEISTY CHICKS
BY KIM K.
DECEMBER 11, 2011